TRAPPED

TRAPPED

S. A. BODEEN

FEIWEL AND FRIENDS

NEW YORK

A FEIWEL AND FRIENDS BOOK
An Imprint of Macmillan

Our books may be purchased for promotional, educational, or business use.
Please contact your local bookseller or the Macmillan Corporate and
Premium Sales Department at (800) 221-7945 ext. 5442 or by e-mail
at MacmillanSpecialMarkets@macmillan.com.

Library of Congress Cataloging-in-Publication Data

Names: Bodeen, S. A. (Stephanie A.), 1965– author.
Title: Trapped / S. A. Bodeen.
Description: First Edition. | New York : Feiwel & Friends, 2016. | Series:
    Shipwreck Island ; 3 | Summary: "It's up to Sarah Robinson to save her
    shipwrecked family from a time-traveling 'curator' of souls and a
    treasure-hunting criminal in Book 3 of the Shipwreck Island series"—
    Provided by publisher.
Identifiers: LCCN 2015026924| ISBN 9781250027818 (hardback) |
    ISBN 9781250086921 (ebook)
Subjects: | CYAC: Shipwrecks—Fiction. | Survival—Fiction. | Stepfamilies—
    Fiction. | Time travel—Fiction. | BISAC: JUVENILE FICTION /
    Action & Adventure / General. | JUVENILE FICTION / Action &
    Adventure / Survival Stories.
Classification: LCC PZ7.B63515 Tr 2016 | DDC [Fic]—dc23
LC record available at http://lccn.loc.gov/2015026924

Book design by Anna Booth

Feiwel and Friends logo designed by Filomena Tuosto

First Edition—2016

1   3   5   7   9   10   8   6   4   2

mackids.com

For Jessi Gile Eaton

1

Sarah Robinson huddled on the cold stone floor of the cavern, stunned that the villainous Curator was, in fact, the small, blond, freckle-faced boy in a blue jumpsuit currently pinned under her stepbrother Marco.

Her heart pounded as she recalled the events of the past few days. First on the list was the unexpected and brutal typhoon that swept their skipper overboard and led to the wreck of the *Moonflight*, marooning them on a place they christened Shipwreck Island. *They* being Sarah's father, John Robinson; his new wife, Yvonna Murillo; and her two boys, Marco and Nacho, along with the skipper's big black dog, a Newfoundland named Ahab.

Then came all the strange things they saw and

heard on the island, leading up to their discovery of an unconscious girl on the beach. When she regained consciousness, Cashmere Bouchard told them how her grandfather Sarge owned a sailboat charter business and was hired by a man and woman who seemed like typical—and snobby—tourists. But the two were secretly hunting for a certain remote island that held a stash of mysterious treasure the man had left behind. Holding Sarge at gunpoint, the couple stranded Cash on Shipwreck Island and said they would come back for her once they found the island they sought.

Cash told the Robinsons that she had fended for herself before being captured by someone called the Curator. After a day or so she escaped, which is when the Robinson family encountered her on the beach. Sarah's dad went looking for the Curator, but didn't return. Then Nacho had gone missing with Ahab as well.

So Marco and Sarah went to find them. Along the way, they'd seen bizarre creatures, including a shark on legs that had nearly made a meal of Sarah's new stepbrother. Then they reached a cavern full of white modules, each with a frosted glass window and an animal inside.

Sarah glanced at the three nearest her and gulped.

Those held something else. And Sarah could do nothing about it while sitting on the floor.

"Marco!"

Sarah sucked in a breath and froze again, afraid to move. Before Marco took control, the blond boy had used a white tube to shoot a net at Sarah, which was stuck to her leg. Cash had warned them about the weapon, so Sarah knew that if the net became entangled with the rest of her, she'd be immobilized.

Marco got to his feet and pointed the tube at the boy, whose eyes remained closed as his chest rose up and down. Marco glanced at Sarah. "Did you see that?"

Marco could only mean one thing: The boy had actually changed *bodies*. When Marco had pinned him to the ground, hands on his throat, the boy first appeared as an elderly man in a jumpsuit, then changed to a red-haired woman, then morphed to a man with chestnut hair. Finally, when Marco threatened to choke the life out of him, he turned into the boy, a shape that seemed to stick longer than the others.

Perhaps this was who he really was. Sarah couldn't be sure about anything anymore.

She nodded in the boy's direction. "What is going on here?"

The boy coughed.

Marco quickly tightened his grip on the weapon.

The boy opened his eyes and slowly sat up. He held his palms out toward Marco.

"Please don't. I mean you no harm."

" 'No harm'?" Marco's eyes narrowed. "Seriously?"

Sarah pointed toward the closest row of white modules, where her father stood motionless, like a specimen in a test tube. "You . . . you froze my dad!"

"And my brother." Marco pointed down the row.

Sarah glanced at the modules, where Nacho and the dog, Ahab, stood in the same kind of cold stasis as her father. A rush of heat made its way up her insides.

"How could you do that?" she cried. She took in the strange scene around her—all those containers, all those animals. "How could you do that to *them*?"

The boy rubbed his throat for a moment as he noticed the net still stuck to Sarah's leg. He told Marco, "Twist the end and you can remove the net."

Marco stepped a few feet away from the boy, until he was next to Sarah. "And why should I trust you?"

"I don't lie," said the boy.

Sarah scowled. "No, you just take innocent people and animals and turn them into . . . into . . . *Popsicles*!"

"But they aren't hurt," protested the boy.

4

"Then let them out!" Sarah shouted.

Marco added, "Yeah. Then let them out."

The boy shook his head.

Marco twisted the end of the white tube and pointed it at Sarah's leg.

She gasped. "No, Marco! Wait! You don't know what—"

But before she could do anything, a puff of steam came out of the tube. Her leg tingled, and as she watched and waited with a pounding heart, the netting dissolved.

Sarah exhaled.

A knife that had been tangled in the net dropped to the floor. Marco picked up the blade, folded it, and put it in his pocket.

Sarah rubbed her leg for a moment, then bent her knee a few times. Convinced that she was truly unharmed, she relaxed and took the hand Marco offered her.

"Okay?" he asked as he pulled her up.

She nodded. "Thanks."

They both glared down at the boy. He darted a few looks their way before lowering his gaze to his feet, which were clad in taupe-colored woven shoes. "I'm not your enemy."

"Then who are you?" asked Marco.

"*What* are you?" asked Sarah.

The boy held out his hand.

Sarah glanced at Marco, then stepped forward and helped the boy up.

"Thank you." He brushed his palms on his blue jumpsuit.

"How did you do that?" asked Sarah. "Change bodies?"

Still looking at his feet, the boy said, "It's a long story."

Marco glanced at the modules. "Are you going to let them out?"

The boy's shoulders slumped. "I . . . can't."

Marco pointed the white tube at the boy. "Then I guess we have time for your story."

Sarah's stomach growled.

Marco rolled his eyes.

"What?" Sarah scowled. "I can't help it."

"You're hungry." The boy's words were quick and pointed, as if he was in a hurry. "I can feed you."

Sarah and Marco exchanged a glance. Cash had told them about the food while she'd been imprisoned. How it had made her fall asleep. Sarah shook her head.

"We're not eating your food. Cash told us you drugged her."

The boy sighed. "Yes, I did. But I won't do that to you."

Neither Sarah nor Marco said anything. Sarah was so hungry that she considered believing him. Actually, she was beyond consideration. She was ready to eat whatever he put in front of her.

The boy said, "I'll sample it first. You can see." He seemed eager as he pointed to one side of the cavern. "Please. Let me show you to my cabin."

"Cabin?" asked Sarah. "Like on a ship?"

The boy nodded. Sarah and Marco glanced at each other as the boy led the way. Marco followed close behind, still brandishing the white tube, while Sarah brought up the rear. She stopped to take one more look behind her, at the modules that encased her dad and stepbrother and the dog.

"I'll get you out," she whispered. "I promise." And then she turned to follow Marco, hoping that she'd be able to keep her word.

2

Marco trod carefully as he followed the boy. He kept the weapon raised; he would be stupid to trust him after what they'd just seen. He didn't believe the boy when he said he couldn't release Nacho and John, as well as Ahab and the other animals. In fact, he found it hard to believe anything the boy said, despite his assurance that he didn't lie.

But Marco suspected that Sarah didn't feel the same way. She was scared—and hungry. They would have to stick together if they were going to free Nacho and John and Ahab.

They left the cavern and continued down a narrow white hallway, the walls and floors made of a shiny, glittery tile like nothing he had ever seen. The air in there smelled much fresher than in the cave. They passed a few doors. Was one of them where Cash had been held? Because the last few moments had proved to Marco that—despite his original feeling to the contrary—the girl they found on the beach had been telling the truth about her ordeal. And this didn't exactly ease Marco's mind.

The boy stopped in front of a door, startling Marco. "You go in," he told the boy. "And don't try anything."

The boy's eyes were sad. "I am not going to try anything." He waved a hand. With a whir, the door slipped open to the side.

"Cool," said Sarah from behind Marco.

Marco locked his gaze on the boy and whispered to Sarah, "He's probably trying to distract us. Help me keep an eye on him."

The boy entered the room.

Sarah followed and whispered back to Marco, "I think you can relax a tad."

But Marco didn't think he should relax, even a little. He took a slow, deliberate step into the room, which was as white as the corridor. Cushioned seats lined the sides, not unlike the seats of the *Moonflight*, and a long table connected to one wall.

The boy walked over to a console and opened something that resembled a microwave. "What are you hungry for?"

Sarah said, "A grilled cheese sandwich."

"Sarah!" said Marco.

She huffed. "What? He asked what I wanted and I told him."

"Like he's gonna have stuff to make grilled cheese." Marco rolled his eyes.

"Cash said he gave her a sandwich." Sarah told the boy, "We met Cashmere, you know. The girl you held here. Did you know that was her name?"

The boy shook his head slightly and shuffled through a stack of shiny discs. He inserted one into the side of the pseudo-microwave and pushed a button. A buzz began and then ended a moment later. The boy opened the door, pulled out a plate, and set it down on the table.

Orange cheese oozed enticingly out from between two perfectly browned pieces of bread. Sarah stuck her tongue out at Marco. "Told you."

The boy slid out a chair for Sarah. She quickly sat down and pulled the plate toward her.

"No." Marco pointed at the boy. "You eat first."

Sarah licked her lips as the boy tore off a chunk of the sandwich, then popped it into his mouth and chewed. He swallowed. "Okay?"

Digging into the sandwich with gusto, Sarah didn't wait for Marco's reply. She spoke with her mouth full. "Ish really good."

Marco's mouth watered as he watched Sarah eat. His empty stomach rumbled. "What else can you make?" he asked.

The boy shrugged. "Whatever you want."

"Cheeseburger. With fries. And ketchup." Marco held his breath.

The boy chose a disc, inserted it, and after a brief buzz, opened the door and pulled out a plate with a steaming cheeseburger and crispy-looking waffle fries, an oblong pool of ketchup off to one side.

Marco's mouth fell open. He sat down before the boy had even set the plate in front of him. Marco took a hefty bite of the cheeseburger and had to shut his eyes as he chewed.

Delicious.

Sarah said, "Don't you want him to try it first?"

Marco's eyes shot open and darted to the boy.

The boy shook his head. "There's nothing in the

food. I promise." He sat down on one of the seats against the wall and watched them eat.

Sarah asked, "What's your name?"

"I'm the Cur—"

"No!" interrupted Marco. "I don't want to hear it. Who are you *really*?"

The boy sighed, as if resigned to finally tell the truth. "My name is Leonis."

"Like the star?" asked Marco.

Sarah raised her eyebrows at him.

Marco shrugged. His stepsister obviously had no idea how impossible it was to live in the same house as Nacho without picking up a fair amount of astronomical knowledge—facts that Marco had considered useless, until now.

The boy nodded. "My mother calls me Leo for short."

"Where are you from?" asked Sarah.

Leo's gaze shifted from Sarah to Marco. "I don't know if you want to know. Or if you're ready to know."

With a full mouth, Marco said, "We're ready."

Leo said, "You won't believe me."

Sarah rolled her eyes. "After the past few days? I'd believe just about anything." She stuffed the last of the grilled cheese in her mouth, and then wiped her greasy hands on her shorts.

Leo stood.

Marco quickly grabbed the white tube from where he'd set it on the table and aimed at the boy's chest.

Leo frowned. "I meant it. I'm not going to try anything." He walked over to a blank wall and waved his hand over it. A large square portion of the wall glowed, then flickered into a screen. Leo deftly touched several lit buttons along the side, and a view of the starry sky appeared.

Marco stopped chewing and stared.

"Cool." Sarah leaned forward and put her elbows on the table.

Leo swiped the screen and the vision zoomed in, revealing one star in particular.

"This is Sirius."

"The Dog Star," said Marco. He took another bite of food.

"Yes. And behind Sirius . . ." Leo swept his hand across the star, and a green-and-blue planet—clearly more blue than green—popped into the space.

"Is that Earth?" asked Sarah.

"No. It's my home."

Marco swallowed, setting down both the tube and what remained of his cheeseburger. "You're an alien."

"Perhaps."

Sarah said, "If you're from outer space, then you're definitely an alien."

"Then I suppose I am." Leo touched the screen and the wall was simply a wall once more. He sat back down. "Like I said, I am not sure you are ready to hear any of this."

"Will you unfreeze my brother and stepdad?" asked Marco.

Leo hesitated, and then shook his head.

"Will hearing all this *help* unfreeze them?" asked Marco.

Leo said, "I don't know. The problem is . . ."

"What?" asked Sarah.

"I need help," said Leo.

"We can help," said Sarah.

Marco nodded.

Leo sighed. "I don't think anyone can."

Marco finished his meal and stood up. "We will. If you unfreeze my brother and her dad."

Sarah nodded. "My dad is smart. He can help."

Marco said, "So can we work out a deal?"

The boy in the blue jumpsuit jumped up. "Yes."

Marco patted the white tube. "No funny stuff."

"Marco, seriously?" said Sarah.

Marco frowned. "What? I don't trust him."

Leo said, "This way."

With Marco right on his heels with the white tube, and Sarah following, Leo led the way out of the room and down the hall, where they left the brightly lit cabin for a dark passageway with a rough stone floor, lit only by torches on the sides.

Marco didn't recognize that part of the cave. "This isn't the way we came."

Leo slowed. "This way is faster." He began to turn left down another passageway, but suddenly leaped to the right and slipped inside a doorway.

"Hey!" Marco lunged for him, then tripped and fell.

Sarah was so close behind that her feet tangled in his and she landed on top of Marco with a nearly breathless "*oomph!*"

The white tube slid from Marco's grasp. He stretched his arm out, trying to grab it.

But Leo snatched it up and leveled it at them.

"You said you didn't lie!" said Sarah.

Marco slowly untangled himself from Sarah and sat up. "I knew we couldn't trust him."

"I'm sorry. There is far too much at stake. I have things to do." Leo backed up so that he stood in the corridor, just outside the doorway.

Marco got to his feet and threw himself at the boy. His head slammed into something hard. He dropped to his knees, clasping his head in his hands. "Ow!"

Sarah set a hand on his shoulder. "You okay?"

"Do I *look* okay?" Marco rubbed his head. "What was that?"

Sarah reached out. Although she didn't see anything, not even glass, a substance lay under her hand that prevented her from exiting the doorway. She glared at the boy. "We were going to help you."

Leo shook his head. "But you cannot. And there is no more time to waste." He paused a moment. "I am sorry I had to lie to you." He turned to go.

"Wait!" yelled Marco. "You can't leave us here. We have to get back to my mom. She's sick."

The boy faced them. He seemed about to say something when Marco felt a rumble under his feet, a rumble that soon intensified.

"It's an earthquake!" shouted Sarah.

Although Marco had never been in an earthquake, he didn't think that's what it was.

Leo froze, his eyes wide as he stared down the corridor.

The ground under their feet shook so hard that Marco could barely stay upright, and lost his footing. He set a hand against the wall to keep from falling.

Sarah began to topple and clutched at him. "Marco! What's happening?" Her eyes widened and her mouth dropped open. She pointed.

Marco shifted to see what had her so spooked. His heart nearly stopped.

The corridor was awash with red light, coming from a crimson ball—exactly the same as the one from the other day—that screamed toward them.

Leo stood right in the menace's path, frozen in place. "Move!" shouted Marco. "Leo!" The boy didn't move. Marco tried once more. *"Leonis!"*

At the last second, as the red missile was nearly upon him, Leo turned, waved his hand, and dove into the room with Marco and Sarah. All of them fell into a scrambled heap.

Marco raised his head in time to see the scarlet flash pass by and continue down the corridor. He untangled his limbs and rolled away from the others. His heart pounded so hard he had to gasp for air. He sat up.

Sarah was on Leo's back, pushing his face into the floor. Her eyes narrowed, her dark bangs smashed onto her forehead with sweat. "No more lying! Tell us the truth!"

Marco was surprised at her strength. Apparently, his stepsister had finally had enough of Leo.

The white tube lay where it had slid across the floor, and Marco quickly retrieved it. He aimed it at the two of them.

Sarah snarled, "Watch where you point that."

"I know." Marco told Leo, "She's right. It's time you told us what's really going on here."

"Fine." Leo's voice was muffled. "I'll tell you everything if you just get her off me."

Marco took one look at the anger spread across Sarah's face and had the feeling that now would not be the time to tell his stepsister to do anything she didn't want to do. He bit his lip.

"Sorry. I don't know exactly how I'm gonna do that."

3

Sarah glared at Marco. There was no way she was going to let that stupid lying alien boy up, even if he had fed her an excellent sandwich. She'd had enough of his lies and didn't appreciate being imprisoned by him, especially *after* they had offered to help him.

She leaned over him. "Let my dad out!"

Half of Leo's face was pressed into the floor, his eyes scrunched up.

Marco walked over and set a hand on Sarah's shoulder. "Let him up."

Sarah pushed harder on the boy. "Not until he promises to let my dad out."

"Come on." Marco brandished the white tube. "He won't do anything while I have this."

Sarah groaned. "Fine." She stood up and stepped aside. "But I want some answers."

Leo climbed to his feet. "Just let me tell you everything and then you'll understand."

Marco cautiously reached a hand through the door, then leaned out into the corridor. "Is that thing coming back?"

Leo shook his head. "It's just a timer."

Sarah's eyes narrowed. "A what?"

"Like a countdown," he said.

"Like an alarm clock?" asked Marco.

Leo shrugged. "That is sort of the alarm."

"Kinda hard to miss," said Sarah.

Leo said, "That's the point."

Marco asked, "What's the countdown for?"

Sarah's stomach did a little flip. She was pretty sure she didn't want to know the answer to that question, and halfway hoped this increasingly annoying alien boy (from behind the Dog Star) wouldn't answer.

Leo said, "I have to tell you the rest of the story first."

"Well, then let's go," said Marco.

"Where?" asked Leo.

Sarah was tired of the cave. She wanted to be in the sun. "Outside."

"As you wish." Leo led the way out the door and down the corridor the way they'd been heading when he tricked them.

Sarah followed. The rocky floor became more uneven, but she saw a light at the end. They stepped out onto the beach and into the glare of the sweltering afternoon sun. The heat seeped in, warming her bones that were still half chilled from the innards of the cave.

Leo put up a hand, shading his face from the glare.

Marco hefted the white tube, pointing it straight at Leo's chest. "You can tell us everything now. But don't expect us to believe any of it."

Sarah was thirsty from her sandwich and wished she had asked for something to drink before they left. She tried to ignore her dry throat because she had more important things to worry about. Like why this strange kid had frozen her dad. And how he would unfreeze him, along with Nacho and Ahab. She found herself feeling slightly relieved that the dreadful Curator was simply a boy, a boy who she could pin on the floor if she wanted. The knowledge made her feel safer somehow.

Leo stopped and faced them. "I know you won't believe me. So let me show you." He held out a hand to Sarah, the other to Marco.

The two looked at each other. Marco shook his head. "I don't trust you."

"I know," said Leo. "But this is the best way to show you."

Sarah gulped. "Marco, you stay over there and watch him." Her heart beat faster as she held out a hand to Leo. "Show me. Show me what you want us to know."

Marco started to protest.

"It'll be okay, Marco." Then, before her stepbrother could stop her, she grabbed Leo's hand.

Instantly, a buzz like an electric current rippled throughout her entire body. Her vision went dark and she gasped. Then, slowly, her sight reappeared, revealing a starry sky, and a tiny blue-and-green marble: Earth, from far away. She felt like she was at a planetarium. A chill drifted over her. Goose bumps blossomed on her arms and legs.

Leo's voice was disembodied, as if it came from inside her head. "A very long time ago my people came to Earth."

Sarah seemed to be in motion, as if on a ship. But she didn't feel sick, like she had on the *Moonflight*.

The hairs on the back of her neck rose. She wasn't alone. Others stood beside her, but didn't react to her presence in the least. The figures were over six feet tall, some closer to seven. They seemed familiar, yet different, and were all dressed in blue jumpsuits. Their faces seemed a bit fuzzy, unfocused. She realized she should have felt afraid, but she didn't.

Was she in some kind of memory? As an observer, not a participant?

Leo asked softly, "Okay so far?"

In her dream state—or whatever it was, she couldn't decide on a name for it—Sarah turned. Leo stood beside her, clearer than the others. To Sarah, he looked no different from anyone she knew. But then, she reminded herself, she had seen him change bodies. So perhaps what she saw on the outside was not all that accurate.

Leo's hand tightened around hers as he continued. "This is my planet." Instantly, she and Leo were no longer on the ship. Instead, they stood on a green hill, looking over a vast body of water.

A lake?

No, bigger than that.

A sea? Even an ocean, perhaps?

A cool wind ruffled the dark strands of hair that had come loose from her braids, tickling her neck. A light mist kissed her skin. "Pretty. It looks like Earth."

Leo kept on. "But it has been around longer and we're further along in every aspect." He pointed at a distant city, with hundreds of tall buildings.

"We have cities too," said Sarah.

"But we are especially advanced in technology. Space travel, for one."

And then they were back on the ship with the others and Sarah felt the motion again. But there was something else as well, as if the beings on the ship were not just on a vacation. She sensed an urgency that something major depended on the journey.

The others seemed to be, she felt, *desperate.*

"When is this?" asked Sarah.

"In your time?" Leo's forehead wrinkled for a moment. "Probably seven hundred years ago."

Sarah swallowed. "Wow."

Leo pulled her over to a glass wall.

Sarah gazed down on Earth, so big and real. She reached out a hand to touch it, but felt only glass.

Leo said, "They chose to disembark on the largest continent."

Sarah pointed to the landform below. "Africa." Suddenly, her stomach leaped as the craft descended. "We're landing there *now?*"

Leo nodded. "This is then."

Sarah gulped. "Seven hundred years ago? In *Africa*?" She racked her brain to remember what she'd learned in history about that time period. Seven hundred years ago, much of the planet was unsettled, wasn't it?

Would anyone they met be friendly?

Leo turned to the wall opposite the glass. A panel slid open. "Come." He led her out of the ship, following some of the others who still seemed not to notice Leo and Sarah. The thick, warm air of the orange African dawn greeted them. Sarah stepped down onto the scrubland. The sand gave way under her feet, feeling as real as any ground she'd ever stood upon.

About a half mile away loomed an enormous reddish-brown cliff that seemed, to Sarah, nearly the height of the Sears Tower. Sarah and her father had gone to the top when they visited Chicago last summer.

Before he had remarried.

Before she had two stepbrothers.

Before this nightmare of a trip.

Sarah sighed.

She gazed to the left and right, unable to see where the behemoth of a landform began or ended.

Not wasting any time, the group began to stride

toward the cliff. Leo and Sarah followed close behind. The acrid smell of woodsmoke drifted toward them on the breeze, and a rooster crowed. She almost smiled at the easily identifiable sound, until she heard something she didn't recognize.

Whump. Whump. Whump.

She had no idea what could be causing the noise, a thought that made her heart speed up. Sarah swallowed. Her throat was so dry. Being nervous made her feel even more parched.

The group stopped, facing the cliff.

Whump. Whump. Whump.

What did they see? Sarah noticed only the steep wall jutting straight up, and the plateau on top. But the others stared at the base of the cliff. They obviously saw something there.

"What are they looking at?" she asked.

Leo pointed. "Don't you see?"

Sarah lowered her gaze in the direction of his arm. Then she gasped. An entire village was built into the side of the escarpment: dwellings made of dull-colored mud that blended perfectly into the color of the cliff, perfectly camouflaged. The homes were box shaped with flat roofs, holes cut out of the walls for windows. They all seemed connected to one another.

Among every few homes perched up off the ground on stilts was a cone-shaped building with a thatched roof. All of the buildings seemed to defy gravity, as if somehow attached to the cliff itself.

As the group headed closer to the village, the rhythmic pounding grew louder.

WHUMP! WHUMP! WHUMP!

Sarah tightened her grip on Leo's hand as her heart beat faster.

The group reached the edge of the buildings and stopped. They blocked Sarah's view, so she leaned out to see around them, hoping that she was as invisible to all of them as she suspected.

Sarah relaxed when she saw the source of the sound: three women pounding long, thick carved wooden rods up and down. "What are they doing?"

"Crushing millet. They make flour from it." Leo pointed to one of the cone-shaped structures. "They store the grain in those."

Suddenly, the women stopped their work and turned to face the group of strangers. One wiped her dark, glistening brow, and then called out. People emerged from the dwellings. A few heads popped up from the roof of a house, as if they'd slept there. A group of laughing children ran out from behind the buildings, barely clothed, their skin sprinkled with dust. They froze, staring with wide, dark eyes at the strangers.

Sarah glanced down at her feet. They were covered in the same dust. Before she could consider how that might be possible, how she could get dirty from a memory, Leo dropped her hand.

She was back on the beach.

Marco stared at Leo with a look of annoyance. "Well? Are you going to show her something or not?"

4

Before Sarah opened her eyes and frowned at him, Marco had watched her and Leo simply stand there and hold hands.

Sarah answered his question. "But he did show me. We were gone forever."

"What are you talking about?" Marco shook his head. "You've been standing right there."

"No!" Sarah sounded frustrated.

Marco could tell she thought he didn't believe her. And he didn't, not at all. She and Leo hadn't done anything except close their eyes and hold hands for a minute or two.

Yet she tried to convince him. "We were on a space-ship. And we landed in Africa."

Marco couldn't help but smile at the absurdity. "Right."

Sarah glared at him before turning to Leo. "Why did you let go of my hand?"

"I want you both to see it." Leo asked Marco, "Are you ready to take a trek in the memories?"

Marco was tired of Leo's delays. He wanted to unfreeze his brother and stepdad, get back to his mom, and figure out how to get off the stupid island. "The only trek I'm taking is back inside to get my brother." He told Sarah, "Let's go."

Before Marco could stop him, Leo grabbed his hand and Sarah's.

Suddenly, Marco found himself next to a soaring cliff, surrounded by people clothed in blue, their faces somewhat blurred. He squinted and tried to get a better look at them as children ran past, stirring up dust that drifted onto his legs.

"See?" Sarah's voice woke him up. She and Leo were in far clearer focus than the people in blue.

Marco asked, "Where are we?"

"Western Africa. About seven hundred years ago," Leo said.

Marco wasn't exactly sure how much he believed.

But that place, that moment, felt so *real* he found it hard *not to* believe.

Adult villagers emerged from some of the dwellings, naked except for coverings on the more private parts of their bodies. Marco stepped closer to one of the structures. The door was wooden, carved so elaborately with figures of people and animals that he couldn't resist reaching out with his free hand to touch it. Why did the carvings seem familiar?

"Wait!" His eyes darted to his feet and he whipped around. "The tube! I lost it!"

Leo said, "It's back at the beach. It wouldn't work here anyway."

Marco relaxed. Strange, but he didn't feel frightened. For some reason, he felt himself trusting the boy from the stars.

An old man with a gray beard walked up to Leo's people and spoke to them. The man appeared to be kind, and seemed to welcome them, although Marco couldn't understand his language.

Sarah said, "They don't seem afraid of you at all."

Leo shook his head. "No. My people were welcomed."

"How did they know the language?" asked Marco.

Leo nodded at his wrist, and a thin black bracelet

Marco hadn't noticed before. "One of our advancements. Almost like an implant that filters our language into anyone else's. And the other way around."

"Cool." Marco stood with Sarah and Leo at the edge of the activity. They observed as the villagers brought some kind of porridge that Leo's people quickly tucked into.

The scene fuzzed up.

With his free hand, Marco rubbed his eyes, but his vision didn't clear. "What's going on?"

Leo said, "There's more I have to show you before you see what happened next."

Sarah screeched.

Marco found himself floating in black space, his limbs weightless and awkward. Chill air rushed around him loudly, stars dazzlingly bright in front of him. His heart pounded.

Marco clutched Leo's hand more tightly, not exactly sure what might happen if he let go. But he *was* certain that he didn't want to find out.

Leo must have sensed their fear, because he reassured them. "We're fine! Look. That star is Sirius."

Marco gulped as they seemed to fly over and around the star. He flutter-kicked and made a lame attempt at half a forward crawl with his free arm, but nothing seemed to help him get control of his body. So he let himself drift, steered along by Leo.

Nacho would have loved it.

And then there was another star that orbited Sirius. Leo said, "This star is invisible from Earth, and its orbit around Sirius takes fifty years."

Suddenly, Saturn streamed past in front of them, resplendent rings so blinding that Marco shielded his eyes with his free arm as he swallowed a scream.

Leo said, "My people told the tribe about Sirius and the star. And about the four moons of Jupiter—"

"*Don't* take us to Jupiter!" shouted Sarah.

Marco was relieved, because he was thinking the same thing. His stomach did flips, and he was afraid he was going to hurl. For the first time, he felt a little empathy for Sarah and her bout of motion sickness on the *Moonflight.*

"These were all things your Earth people hadn't even discovered yet." Leo dropped their hands.

They were back on the beach.

Marco took a deep breath. The white tube was still in his hand, which was now trembling. "This sounds familiar. Nacho made me watch this show with him once."

"I wouldn't think Nacho could ever make you do anything," said Sarah.

Marco shrugged. "He was sick. I felt bad for him."

Sarah raised her eyebrows. "That was nice."

Marco ignored her mild surprise and continued. "This tribe in Africa never had contact with anyone until some anthropologists showed up in the 1930s. And the tribe had these wild myths, how they'd been visited by beings from an advanced culture."

Sarah asked, "Did they believe them?"

Marco shook his head. "Not at first. But they knew about the four moons of Jupiter and the rings of Saturn." He shivered slightly, remembering how close he had just been to that planet, even if it hadn't actually been real.

Had it?

"Someone could have told them," said Sarah.

"Yeah," said Marco. "But then they spoke about Sirius B."

"What's that?" asked Sarah.

Leo spoke up. "The object we saw orbiting Sirius."

Marco nodded. "And it wasn't photographed until 1970. But the tribe knew about it long before then." He met Leo's gaze.

Leo smiled a little. "Because they had been told by my people."

Something nagged at Marco, some other detail from

the show that he couldn't quite remember, something even odder than the rest. He wished Nacho were there. His brother would know.

Sarah asked Leo, "But that was it? They told the tribe some stuff and went back home?"

"Not exactly. My people were on a mission."

Sarah glanced at Marco, who asked, "What kind of mission?"

"Our planet is very similar to Earth," said Leo.

"You already showed me that." Sarah looked down at the sand.

Marco wondered if she had the same weird feeling about Leo that he did. Because the boy was obviously on some kind of mission himself.

Leo said, "Your planet has limited resources. Which your people are beginning to realize."

Sarah said, "Nacho explained to me about the exo-planets." She bit her lip. "He would be excited to learn that it's all true. But he's not here."

Marco frowned. His little brother *was* there, just not able to walk or talk or be with them, because he was frozen. His frustration bubbled up. "Can you get to it? Tell us why my brother is frozen and you can't let him out?"

Leo glanced over at Marco and sidled away from

him slightly. "The history of my people *is* getting to it." He reached up and wiped sweat off his face, then took a deep breath. "This is what you may find hard to believe. Because your civilization isn't there yet. But my people created the *progenitor.*"

"What's that?" asked Sarah.

"It allowed us to replicate whatever we wanted." Leo walked down toward the water. He took off his shoes and let a wave lap up over his feet.

Sarah followed him. "You probably shouldn't get that close to the water."

Marco caught up too. "I don't get it. You can just *make* whatever you want? Like the grilled cheese?"

Leo backed away from the water a bit and stepped back into his shoes. "The food center on my ship was created from the same technology."

Sarah asked, "What else could you replicate besides food?"

Leo shrugged. "Objects. Plants. Animals. Whatever we chose."

Marco thought out loud, "So it's like a 3-D printer."

"Only times like a million!" added Sarah. "How cool is that."

"There were problems." Leo scratched his head. "It

36

was so much power and caused fights over who should control it. Eventually, the leaders decided it was too much power for anyone to have. So they split it in two."

Sarah snapped her fingers. "You left half on Earth."

Leo smiled at her. "Yes. We entrusted the tribe with it."

"But why give it to them?" asked Marco. "I mean, seven hundred years ago there were other more advanced civilizations."

"But we weren't seeking the most *advanced*." Leo held up a finger. "Do you know one of the most important pillars of that tribal society?"

Marco shrugged.

"Harmony." Leo explained, "The power to create walks hand in hand with the power to destroy. We needed a hiding place for half of the progenitor. But not just to keep it safe. To keep your planet safe from its powers. In the wrong hands, it could be a weapon." Leo looked down at his feet. "As we learned."

"Is that what happened on your planet?" asked Marco.

Leo lifted his chin. "Yes. Until then my society had been content, peaceful, and harmonious. But the creation of the progenitor caused a rift. One that could not be fixed."

"What happened?" asked Sarah.

Goose bumps rose on Marco's arms as Leo reached for their hands. "This is one of the parts you aren't going to like."

5

Afraid of what she was going to see, Sarah closed her eyes and focused on her hand in Leo's. At first his touch had seemed weird—she didn't go around holding hands with boys, especially not alien boys—but now she found it comforting, especially given his warning. At least she knew that she had only to let go in order to stop the memory and return to the beach.

A cool wind blew into her face. She opened her eyes. They stood on the same green hill on Leo's planet as before, overlooking the same body of water. The scene was calm and serene. In the distance, the buildings loomed, like they had earlier.

Leo told Marco, "This is my planet."

"Looks like Earth," said Marco.

Sarah didn't understand. "It's the same as before."

"Wait." Leo sighed.

An intense light burst across the entire sky, like a camera flash, only so ablaze that Sarah had to scrunch her eyes shut. The fiery stream was followed by a roar, and then a furnace blast of heat.

Sarah shoved her face in her elbow and shouted over the roar, "I'm scared!"

"It can't hurt us!" shouted Leo.

She opened her eyes.

A gigantic cloud of smoke climbed over the city, brilliant streaks of yellow and red shooting through. The formation ascended rapidly, folding over and over, like cake batter in a mixer. Her jaw dropped as the cloud continued to rise, reaching miles into the sky until the sides spilled over.

Sarah's hands trembled and her stomach clenched. She knew what that thing was. *A mushroom cloud.*

Her mother's grandparents, Sarah's great-grandparents, had been children in Japan in 1945. Just last year her dad told Sarah the stories, about Hiroshima and Nagasaki, and the ghastly horrors caused by an atomic bomb. But, before now, she had only seen the gruesome pictures.

Sarah wished the moment could be unseen, a wish she knew couldn't ever come true.

She lowered her eyes to the water.

Leo let go of their hands.

They were back on the sand.

Marco shook his head. "Your people built a bomb too."

Sarah glanced at Marco. She hadn't suspected that he would even know about things like nuclear weapons. There was probably a lot more to him than she had ever realized.

The three stood in a circle on the beach. No one said anything, the only sound the quiet whooshing of the waves onto the shore. Sarah thought about the destruction in Japan, long ago. Even though she figured she already knew the answer, she asked, "What happened to the city?"

"Destroyed," said Leo.

"What about the other ones?" asked Marco.

Leo's forehead wrinkled. "The other what?"

"Cities?" Marco scratched his head. "I mean, the bomb destroyed two cities here on Earth. What about your planet?"

Leo stared down at the sand. "One thing I didn't

tell you about my planet. It is very much like Earth, except for the far smaller size. That city you saw was the only one."

Sarah felt her stomach sink. "What happened to your people? And the land? And the animals?" She knew the answer already, but hoped she was wrong.

"The people and animals on the land, gone. Plants, trees, gone. Everything destroyed." Leo's eyes filled with tears.

She wished, for Leo's sake, that she had been wrong. Sarah set a hand on Leo's arm. "How are you here?"

"There's something else I haven't told you," said Leo.

"Is this another thing we won't like?" asked Marco.

Leo sniffled. Half of his mouth curled up. "That all depends." Then the near smile left his face as he stiffened and dropped to his knees. "No!" He covered his face with his hands. "Not now!"

"Leo?" Sarah grabbed the boy's arm and tried to pull him up. But he jerked out of her grasp and scrambled away on his hands and knees. He let loose with an anguished cry.

"Leo!" Marco took a step toward him.

A shimmer surrounded the boy in the jumpsuit.

Marco reached out, as if to touch it.

"Don't!" Sarah grabbed hold of his shirt and yanked. "Come on!"

They backed off a little way down the beach.

The shimmer around Leo intensified, rendering him a mere blurry outline.

"Marco! What's happening?" cried Sarah.

"I don't know!" Marco pushed Sarah slightly behind him.

She was content to stay there, somewhat protected as she peeked around at the whirling space that seemed about to consume Leo.

Leo threw his head back.

Then, the wail came, the wail they had heard the day before and the day before that. Only this time, the sound was deafening.

Sarah crushed her hands over her ears. The cacophony seeped through, vibrating down her entire body. Her knees gave out and she dropped to the sand. She bent over and cradled her head in her arms, trying to shut out the harsh and horrible sound.

Marco landed beside her. She leaned into him. They huddled together as the sound got louder and louder. Sarah never thought in a million years she'd admit it, but she was so glad her stepbrother was with her, so glad to not be alone.

Sarah wasn't even aware when the silence began, because that sound echoed and echoed and echoed. Her skin still tingled. But she felt a nudge in her side and peeked out under her elbow.

Marco was on his knees, ears covered by his hands. He slowly lowered them. "I think it's over."

Sarah sat up.

Leo lay on his side, facing away from them, only his jumpsuit-clad back and legs in view. She started to get up.

Marco grabbed her arm. "I remembered something."

"What?" She waited.

"Remember I saw that show about the tribe? And the alien visitors?"

Sarah nodded.

"There was something I couldn't remember and it's been bugging me this whole time. I think I know what it is." Marco glanced over at Leo, and then lowered his voice. "They described the alien visitors as . . ."

"What?" asked Sarah.

"Amphibious creatures." Marco bit his lip.

"What?" Sarah shook her head, not really under-standing. "Amphibious. You mean like . . . alligators?"

"No." Marco shook his head. "Just, that they live underwater or something."

"Mermaids?" Sarah could believe a lot, especially after all she'd seen so far, but *that* was sincerely pushing it.

Marco shrugged. "I don't know. I'm going to ask Leo."

They both got to their feet and walked over to the boy.

Still on his side and motionless, Leo had his back to them.

Sarah knelt a few feet away. "Do you think that sound hurt him somehow?"

"I don't know," said Marco. "It seemed to come *from* him."

Sarah leaned forward and gently grasped Leo's shoulder. She pulled him toward her.

The boy rolled onto his back on the sand.

She gasped.

Along either side of his face, gills reached all the way back to his ears, which had shrunk to tiny holes. His eyes opened and one hand reached out and held her arm. Webs stretched between each finger.

Only then did Sarah let out a scream to rival the wail they'd all just lived through.

6

Marco fell back on the sand.

Leo sat up, blinking at them, the eyelids sliding slowly from side to side, like some kind of freakish lizard.

Sarah jumped to her feet and backed away, hands covering her mouth.

"What?" Leo glanced down at his webbed fingers and held out his hands. "I suppose you want to know about this."

Marco nodded.

Leo wobbled a bit as he got to his feet. Slowly the webs between his fingers disappeared, as did the gills on his face.

Leo was, once again, the boy from before.

Sarah shot Marco a wide-eyed look.

Leo said, "The reason my people survived the bomb on my planet? We weren't on the land." He paused.

"You were in the water," said Marco.

Leo nodded. "My ancestors stole the progenitor and took to the waves. Not to use it. They planned to hide it, forever, to stop the fighting. But those who remained on the land didn't know where it went and the factions there began to fight. When the bomb went off, my ancestors left our planet."

"Wait," said Sarah. "When did they leave?"

Leo sighed. "In your time? Seven hundred years ago."

"When did they go back?" asked Marco.

Leo slowly shook his head. "They didn't."

"Why?" asked Sarah.

"The planet was ruined," said Leo. "My people have been a lost people ever since. They left half of the progenitor with the tribe so that no one could ever fight over it again. After that, we've been wandering on our ship, waiting until it is time to return home."

"But you showed us your planet!" said Sarah. "And you've never been there?"

Leo shook his head. "I share the memories of my people." He waved a hand in front of his face. "And I share the same cells. We can manipulate them, appear to be more human than we truly are. I can look like any of them, my parents, grandparents—how they look when they appear to be human—when I want to. When you first saw me in the cavern, I was scared. It was just natural for me to change my appearance." Leo seemed apologetic.

"Is that why the people in blue were out of focus? You didn't want us to see what they really looked like?" asked Sarah.

Leo nodded. "They appeared as themselves to the tribe. And they were accepted, treated as beings to be worshipped. I didn't think you were ready to see me as me." He hung his head. "So I appeared as this, to look like you."

Marco swallowed. He didn't want to admit it, but Leo was right about that. His distrust of Leo would have run deeper if he'd first appeared in his true shape. He shot a glance at Sarah.

She looked a little ashamed, like she was thinking the same thing. "But what was that sound?"

"The Cry of the Ancients." Leo continued, "When

it strikes, the force is too powerful to maintain this appearance." He waved a hand in front of his human face. "After my ancestors left our planet, they grieved for their home. They didn't want to forget. They didn't want their descendants to forget. So every day at the same time, we grieve as one. To remember."

"And that will go on forever?" asked Sarah.

"There's one way for it to stop. The only way." Leo turned his face skyward. "If we return to our planet. That will finally end our grief."

"I can't believe you've never even been to your own planet," said Sarah.

"I was born on the ship. That's all I've ever known," said Leo.

"But isn't it safe after all this time?" asked Sarah. "Why didn't you all go back home?"

Leo said, "We've been preparing to return."

"When are you going back?" asked Marco.

Leo's eyes shifted toward the entrance to the cave. "Maybe never, now that my grandfather . . ." His words faded.

Sarah asked, "The bald man? Was he your grandfather?"

Leo nodded. "And the other man was my father."

"And the woman?" asked Marco.

"My mother." Leo's eyes filled with tears.

Marco felt bad for him. "Where are they?"

"My parents stayed on our main ship." He pointed to the sky. "But my grandfather and I came down in this annex." He gestured behind him, at the entrance to the cavern.

"Why did you come to this island?" asked Sarah.

Leo shook his head. "We didn't at first. My grandfather took a small shuttle to retrieve the other half of the progenitor."

Marco was confused. "Why?"

"It was time to go back to our planet. The leaders decided we required the progenitor to make our planet whole again. To replicate the plants, the trees, the animals." Leo stopped.

"What happened?" asked Sarah.

"He went back to Africa, to our friends. But the progenitor had been taken. Stolen." Leo wiped tears away. "Grandfather tracked it to this island. But then the trail went cold. So he came back to the main ship. And he and the other leaders devised a new plan to get what we needed for our planet."

"You came back to take animals," said Marco.

Leo said, "Yes. And plants and trees. And soil."

"Why can't your other ship come and get you?" asked Sarah.

"After all these years, our fuel resources are depleted. There is barely enough for the main ship to return to our planet. Time is running out. If I don't return with this part of the ship, I'll have to stay here. Forever." Leo sighed.

"Why can't you go back?" asked Marco.

"This section of the ship operates by automatic return, which will only work if the preprogrammed containers are full." He pointed back at the cave. "That's what the red fireballs count down. I have less than two days to fill the containers." He put his face in his hands. "Or I can never leave here."

Something occurred to Marco. "Can you tell us what the progenitor looks like?"

Leo looked up. "The tribe encased it in something. I'm unsure what, although it might bear symbols of my people."

Marco pictured the chest he'd saved from the *Moonflight*. The symbols were very similar to the markings on the modules in the cave. What if he passed off the chest as the holder of Leo's lost technology? Maybe he could bargain for Nacho and John and Ahab! He swallowed. "I think I know where it is."

Leo's face grew pale. "What?"

Sarah raised her eyebrows at Marco but didn't say anything.

Marco decided to take a risk. "Unfreeze my brother and I'll tell you what I know."

Leo shook his head. "You're lying."

"I swear," said Marco. "We have a wooden chest. It's carved with the same symbols as the modules inside." He firmed up his grip on the tube. "If you want to see it, you'll let my brother out."

Sarah's gaze locked on Leo's. "But you told us that you can't let them out."

Leo's gaze shifted from Sarah to Marco. "I'll let one go."

"My dad!" Sarah grabbed Marco's shirt. "It has to be my dad! He knows more. He can help."

Marco swallowed and tightened his grip on the tube. He didn't trust Leo to follow through even if they *did* have the progenitor. This might be his one chance to get Nacho back, and he was going to take it, even though it meant lying. "My brother. Unfreeze him and I'll give you the progenitor."

7

"No!" Sarah grabbed for the tube in Marco's hands.

"Sarah, don't!" He elbowed her aside.

She fell in the sand. "Why do you get to decide? I want my dad!" Sarah jumped back up. Why did Marco have to be so selfish? He only got his way because he had the weapon.

And Leonis. Stupid alien liar. He could have unfrozen her dad at any time.

"Let's go." Marco pointed the tube at the entrance.

Leo went first.

Marco shot a look at Sarah.

She scowled and brushed by him.

But he grabbed her arm and whispered, "We can see how he does it and maybe get your dad out too."

"Let go." Sarah yanked her arm out of his grip and stomped down the stone corridor after Leo. She didn't believe that Marco had that in mind when he chose Nacho. Not at all. He only said it so she wouldn't be mad. Well, *surprise*. It didn't work. She felt stupid that she hadn't thought of the chest first. Of trying to convince Leo it was his missing whatchamacallit.

But she would think of something else. No way was she leaving there without her dad. *Unfrozen.*

They reached the cavern, which was bright as day. The sight of the modules, and the knowledge of their purpose, sent a shiver down Sarah's spine. She ran ahead and stopped at the module that contained her dad. One look at the tan legs and the khaki shorts and the polo shirt told her nothing had changed. Except that the fog on his glasses was rapidly freezing over.

She set a hand on the glass and whispered, "I'll get you out first. They don't know it, but I will." She whirled around. "Leo. Why did you freeze my dad instead of keeping him prisoner like Cash?"

Leo seemed a bit taken aback and didn't answer right away.

Marco frowned. "Yeah, why did you?"

Leo's eyes went to the ceiling. "The atmosphere in my ship, in here, is different from that of your Earth."

Marco shot a glance at Sarah. "We're breathing fine."

"For now." Leo dropped his gaze. "I don't know what prolonged exposure will do. It was safer to freeze your father than—"

"It would be safer to just let him go!" Sarah's hands turned to fists.

Marco held up his palm at her. "You're not helping."

Sarah crossed her arms and glared at him.

Marco said to Leo, "Cash was here longer. Nothing's wrong with her."

Leo didn't answer.

"Right?" asked Marco. "Nothing's wrong with Cash, is there?"

Leo ignored him and held a hand over the keypad on Ahab's module.

"I thought you were going to unfreeze his *brother*," said Sarah.

Leo said, "I will. But I haven't done this before. It might be better to practice on the dog in case something goes wrong."

Sarah didn't want to know all the things that could go wrong. She also didn't want anything to happen to Ahab. "Can't you practice on another animal?" She swept her hand to her side toward the other modules.

Leo shook his head. "Those modules were filled a

while ago. The freezing process is complete in less than an Earth day. After that . . ."

Sarah's stomach clenched. "What? What happens?"

"The modules remain locked until they reach my planet."

Her gaze shot back to her frozen father. "Then you have to let him out!"

"We have a deal." Leo told Marco, "I'll practice on the dog. Then I'll let your brother go." He glanced at Sarah. "You'll get your father back once I have the progenitor."

Sarah's throat grew thick and tears welled up. How did this happen? She had gone from being annoyed by new brothers to worrying about her dad being taken by aliens. When Leo found out the chest from the *Moonflight* wasn't what he needed, that Marco lied, the alien would go back on the deal before her dad was freed. She wanted her dad out now. She didn't want him to end up on Leo's planet.

And, as much as she tried to shove the feeling down, Sarah wanted her dad to be there for Yvonna, who maybe needed him just as much as she did.

Sarah brushed away a tear.

No, she needed to stop thinking about *them*. She needed to focus on what was best for *her*. She didn't want to be left alone. And it was clear that, without her dad, she *was*.

Marco was only out for himself and Nacho and their mom. She almost told Leo that Marco was a liar, that the chest was just something stupid Marco had found. But she wanted Marco to go through with the betrayal. It was exactly what she needed. Because, as soon as her dad was unfrozen, she would tell him how Marco had chosen Nacho over him. And once they were all off the island, she would never have to see the Murillo family again.

Marco moved closer. "Let's go. Do this."

Sarah sniffled and wiped her eyes. Was Marco trying to watch Leo's every move, to see what he did so he could copy it? Had he been telling her the truth?

Maybe she believed him, maybe she didn't.

Leo's hand went over the keypad. Slowly, it morphed to a hand with webbing between the fingers. He pressed it onto the keypad.

Sarah frowned. "Why didn't you need webbed hands in the cabin, for the other screen?"

Leo said, "That simpler technology only requires a touch. These have an identity component. I must be myself—my real self—when I touch it."

Sarah's heart sank. If webbed hands were a necessity, they had no chance of repeating his movements.

The glass front slid open.

Hssssssssssss.

Goose bumps raced up Sarah's arms and the sudden chill sent a shiver through her entire body. She held a hand out at arm's length. Invisible in the thick fog.

Something furry and cold brushed against her bare legs.

She screeched.

The mist cleared instantly.

"Ahab!" Sarah set a hand on the dog's head. "Are you okay?"

As if to answer, Ahab jumped up, put his paws on her shoulders, and licked the tears off her face.

Sarah gently pushed him down and brushed off the bits of ice clinging to his fur. "Good boy." She was glad to have at least one ally back.

Marco said, "Now my brother."

Sarah watched, helpless. If only there was something she could do to help her dad.

Leo stepped to the front of Nacho's module and settled his webbed hand on the control panel.

Again, the glass panel slid open.

Hssssssssssss.

Sarah held tight to Ahab's collar as the mist enveloped them. Ahab whined. "It's okay, boy."

A few seconds later, the mist was gone.

Nacho stood there in his purple shirt and khaki shorts, bits of white on the very tips of his brown hair. He blinked. A few flecks of frost flew from his eyelashes. "What happened?"

Marco threw his arms around his little brother.

A new wave of tears hit Sarah. She wanted to have her dad's arms around her. She dropped her hold on Ahab and ran to the module that contained her dad, pounding on the glass with both fists. "Let him out!"

Marco grabbed her arm. "Sarah, we'll get him out."

She whirled around. "I want him out now."

"No!" Leo hadn't raised his voice before, and they all turned to look at him.

Nacho asked, "Who is that?"

Sarah narrowed her eyes at the alien boy. "His name is Leo. He's the Curator that Cash told us about."

Nacho stepped over to Sarah and stared inside the module that housed John Robinson. "Your dad's frozen?"

Marco said, "So were you. Don't you remember?"

Nacho shook his head. "I was on the beach and Ahab ran ahead of me, around the corner. He barked and then he squealed. And then nothing. So I ran toward him and then suddenly I was all wrapped up in some kind of spider's web and couldn't move and then . . ." He frowned. "Wait a second. Why were you hugging me?"

Marco set a hand on Nacho's head. "Because I'm glad to see you."

"Since when?" asked Nacho.

Marco grinned. "Since I like you better when you aren't an ice cube."

"That is *so* awesome for you both." Sarah glared at him.

Nacho asked, "Can we get your dad out now?"

"No." Sarah glanced at Marco. "Leo won't let him out."

"Why not?" asked Nacho.

Leo crossed his arms. "Because we have a deal."

Marco told Leo, "Maybe you should show Nacho what you showed us."

Leo reached for Nacho's hand.

Nacho stepped back.

Marco grabbed Nacho's arm. "Just let him show you."

Nacho glanced at Sarah.

Sarah nodded.

Still looking skeptical, Nacho let Leo take his hand. The two stood there a moment, eyes closed.

Sarah understood why Marco didn't believe Leo had shown her anything at first, because Leo and Nacho appeared to do nothing at all.

A moment later, Leo let go of his hand.

Nacho's eyes opened and grew wide. Then he grinned and shouted, "I knew it!" He jumped up and down a few times, and then stopped to point at Marco. "I told you! I told you." He put his hands on his hips. "We are *so* not alone."

8

Marco didn't even care about Nacho's gloating. He was glad to have his brother back. Part of him felt bad about leaving his stepdad frozen, but for the moment, there was nothing he could do about that. And until he could, he would just have to deal with Sarah. He hoped he could come up with a different plan to get the alien to help them before Leo discovered the truth, that he'd lied about the chest. He forced a smile on his face. "We better get going."

They traipsed out of the cavern and down a stone corridor that quickly led to the beach. The sun felt amazing after the clammy cave, and Marco turned his face skyward for a moment to soak in the warmth.

Sarah trudged at the back.

Marco decided to try to get some answers from Leo. "What is with the weird stuff on this island? There are so many trees that don't belong. And those freaky *animals*."

Nacho looked at Marco and then Leo. "What freaky animals?"

Leo didn't answer. "It will take too long to explain."

"Then show us," said Nacho. "It'll only take a minute, right?"

Leo stopped and held out his hands. Marco set the tube down and took one, Nacho took the other. He turned and held out his free hand to Sarah. "Leo wants to show us something."

Sarah scowled at the three boys. Then, she grasped Nacho's and Marco's hands, completing the circle and thrusting them into another one of Leo's memory treks.

The sounds of rushing water greeted them as they stood on the bank of a pool, under a gushing waterfall. Marco recognized it. "We swam here this morning." But it seemed much longer ago than that.

Around them was nothing but sand. And farther away, a cliff. Marco wondered whether that was where they'd seen the face rock. The day dimmed to night, and above them the stars pressed down. One, brighter than the rest, descended, and landed in the middle of the island.

"My ship," said Leo.

"Cool!" cried Nacho.

A green mountain grew up around the glowing oblong spaceship, hiding it under the newly minted volcano. "I'll speed up this next part," said Leo.

A hum surrounded them, and the night sky quickly swirled overhead, as if on fast-forward. The sun rose and set, the stars whirled above them, countless days and nights raced by.

Marco felt dizzy.

Suddenly, trees of every type—maple, oak, palm, peach—sprouted from the empty ground, and the jungle quickly enclosed the four of them.

Marco could only watch as the days and nights continued to speed by. "What is this?"

Leo said, "Grandfather used his half of the progenitor to speed up the growth. We needed the plants and trees to seed for us to take them back."

Marco spoke his thoughts aloud. "So that's why that creep on Cash's boat didn't recognize the island. You changed it."

Leo led them along the bank of the stream and into a clearing.

Before them stood the little cabin they'd seen earlier, only the stairs and porch were pristine and dust-free, the curtains on the windows clean and straight—far from the decrepit place he'd been inside. Marco shivered, remembering the red bird.

Leo said, "We built this. My grandfather wanted me to be off the ship."

"Had you ever been off the ship before?" asked Marco.

Leo shook his head. "My parents wanted me to have a chance to stand on land in case . . ." He trailed off.

"In case what?" asked Sarah.

"In case this mission didn't work and we didn't make it back home." Leo waved a hand around. "We lived here. We grew things. Grandfather traveled with the ship to collect every animal species he could. He chose this island as a base because no one ever came here."

Marco said, "That's why there are so many trees that don't belong here." He wanted to bring up the animals again, but had the feeling Leo would get to that.

Leo nodded. "We've been here for over a year, growing different things, making sure we can help them survive on our planet." He pointed out to sea. "My grandfather and I have been finding everything our planet needs to start again."

"You mean *taking* what you need," said Sarah.

"Yes." Leo faced Sarah. "But don't you see? If we can fix our planet, we can help you fix yours. If that time ever comes."

Sarah and Marco exchanged a glance. Marco wanted to say that things here would never come to that, but realized there was truth to Leo's words.

Nacho obviously knew it too, because he said, "You mean like climate change. The icebergs are melting. The bees are dying."

"Well, thanks for that picker upper," said Sarah.

Nacho shrugged. "Just being honest." He turned to Leo. "So what happened?"

Leo stared down at his feet. "Growing the plants and trees went well. So did the collection of the animals. But then Grandfather realized he couldn't find them all."

Leo's eyes glittered with tears. "On our ship, each container was already prepared for each species. But when we'd finished, there were still empty containers."

"What was supposed to go in the empty ones?" Marco's throat felt thick, and he didn't want to know the answer.

Leo recited, "The Tasmanian tiger. The passenger pigeon. The Steller's sea cow. The—"

Nacho interrupted. "Those are all extinct."

"We figured that out," said Leo.

"Why didn't you just go home?" asked Sarah. "You must have hundreds of species."

"The ship is programmed to take off when those containers are full. And communication between my home ship and here is disrupted by the solar flares of your sun."

Marco asked, "I thought your technology was advanced."

"It is," said Leo. "But our power sources are limited. If we used any more for communication, to overcome the disruption, we'd lose life support. Plus fuel we need to get home. We have no way to tell them that we can't complete our mission. So Grandfather did the one thing he'd been told not to do."

"What was that?" asked Sarah.

"He tried to replicate with only half the progenitor."

Leo released their hands.

Memory over. They were back at the beach.

Leo wandered down to the edge of the water and gazed out onto the waves. The sun was bright, reflecting off the water.

The boy looked so forlorn that Marco felt bad. He picked up the weapon, then went and stood beside Leo. He reached into his pocket and extended his hand out flat, revealing the perfume flacon.

Leo gasped and slowly reached out for it. He took off the top and inhaled. Although Marco didn't hear them, he knew the words that Leo absorbed. *Please come back.*

"My mother gave this to me when we left the ship. When I had to leave the cabin so fast, I forgot it." Leo's fingers closed around it. "Thank you."

Sarah joined them. "Why did you have to leave so suddenly?"

Leo said, "There's one more thing to show you."

"Are we going to like it?" asked Nacho.

Leo shook his head. "No. Not at all."

9

Sarah was willing to bet that whatever happened next would not be pleasant to witness.

Ahab barked in the direction of the trees at the edge of the beach.

Sarah dropped to her knees beside him. "You're fine."

But the dog began to growl.

Something crashed in the underbrush.

Marco grabbed Sarah and pulled her up. "We need to go!"

Leo and Nacho ran farther down the beach, hugging the tree line. Sarah grabbed Ahab's collar, but he wouldn't budge.

Marco said, "Sarah, come on!"

"I'm not leaving him!" She yanked on Ahab's collar again.

Marco grabbed the dog's collar too. Finally, Ahab relented and ran with them as they caught up to the other two, who had ducked into the woods.

Leo dodged in between a couple of thick tree trunks. "This way!"

Sarah was nearly breathless when they reached a thick stand of bamboo. Leo slid in and they followed.

Sarah dropped to her knees on the ground, arms around Ahab. The others joined her in the hiding place.

Marco held a finger to his lips.

The crashing continued, growing louder as it neared them.

Sarah's heart pounded. The boys all had wide eyes, and their chests heaved from their dash off the beach.

All was silent.

A snorting noise cut the air.

Ahab growled low in his throat.

Sarah set a hand on his head to try to calm him.

Marco held the weapon up as if he planned to use it.

Leo set a hand on Marco's arm and vigorously shook his head.

Marco lowered the weapon and set it aside. Then

he crawled forward and peered out through a gap. He beckoned to them. Slowly, Leo and Nacho joined him.

Sarah held Ahab's collar with both trembling hands. She didn't want to know what made that sound. Whatever creature was out there probably wanted to eat them.

Nacho gasped and covered his mouth.

After another snort, the crashing started up again. Everyone was still as the noise began to retreat. The boys sat up.

His eyes huge, Nacho whispered, "That looked like a rhinoceros with a unicorn horn!"

Sarah glanced at Marco.

He nodded. "Our rhinocorn." He turned to Leo. "Where did it come from?"

It sounded as if the rhinocorn was tearing branches from trees. Leo whispered, "Well, we're stuck here until that thing goes away. I might as well show you." He held up his hands.

Sarah grabbed his hand and held her free hand to Nacho. Nacho took it and held out his hand to Marco, who took it and hesitated for a moment before holding out his other hand to Leo, waiting for the boy from the stars to complete the circle.

Sarah felt a lurch as Leo connected with all of them.

They stood in the clearing by the little cabin from before. The sun was hot. A slight breeze rippled the leaves of a nearby palm tree. A bald man knelt on the ground, his back to them as he seemed to struggle with something.

He stood up and faced them. The man had gills, tiny ears, and webbed fingers.

Nacho sucked in a sharp breath.

Leo's hand stiffened in Sarah's as the door opened. He marched down the stairs, only he wasn't their Leo. He was the Leo from the stars, with gills and webbed hands like his grandfather's.

Leo spoke softly. "Grandfather had begun to try and replicate creatures to fill the empty modules so our ship would take us back to our people."

Leo's grandfather held something in his hand. Sarah squinted, trying to see what it was, but like some of the other memories, the object was blurred.

"Only the eyes of my people can look directly at the progenitor. I'm protecting you," said Leo.

Sarah focused on the bald man's hands. A moment later, a flutter of feathers flew from them. Red feathers. Four wings flapped as the bird took flight.

Marco said, "My bird!"

Sarah gasped. "You made all those weird creatures?"

"You've seen others?" asked Leo.

Sarah blew out a breath. The image of that shark on crocodile legs rushing toward Marco flashed in her mind. She shivered. "We got a very good look, believe me."

"Why did they turn out so . . . freaky?" asked Nacho.

Leo said, "With only half the progenitor, my grandfather was guessing."

Marco asked, "But did you even see if it would work? Putting them in the modules?"

"Tricking the codes?" Leo nodded. "We tried. But the technology is smarter than we are."

Sarah asked, "Then how did you get my dad and Nacho and Ahab in the modules?"

Leo said, "There were some blanks. In case we discovered species our people were unaware of. So I put them in and set the lock and . . ."

Marco said, "And it's just like the other codes."

Leo nodded. "None of the extras count for the final tally."

Sarah was about to ask if her dad counted for the final tally when a black squirrel with a red-and-white-striped tail brushed by Sarah's leg. She screeched. "So you just let them run around the place?"

Leo's eyes narrowed. "No. We didn't just let them run around." He let go of her hand and Marco's.

The four of them were seated, surrounded by bamboo, as if they'd never left.

The rhinocorn still rustled around nearby.

A fat tear slipped down Leo's cheek and he brushed it away. He sighed. "Grandfather would make one creature at a time. I'd shoot a net to immobilize it, then we'd take it to the cave to see if a module would accept it."

"What did you do with the ones that didn't work?" Nacho pointed toward the noises. "Like *that* one."

Marco said, "Nacho, I think he's trying to tell us that *none* of them worked."

Leo shook his head. "But we kept trying. And my grandfather made a valley for them."

Marco glanced at Sarah. "We saw that too." He cleared his throat. "But some of them weren't in the valley."

"I know." Leo was quiet for a moment.

Sarah set a hand on the boy's arm. "Show us what happened."

Once more, the four joined hands.

But this time, instead of the clearing by the cabin,

they were deeper in the woods. Leo's grandfather was hunched over the same blurred object as before.

The other Leo, the alien version, clutched a white tube aimed straight at the old man.

His grandfather said, "I know the last one got away, but this one will be slower." His voice was calm and reassuring.

"I'm ready." Leo narrowed his eyes and tightened his grip on the weapon.

A hum began. The vibrations increased until they rippled down Sarah's neck. Suddenly, a flash of black fur burst from the object.

Sarah gasped.

A black panther crouched before them, with a beard of scarlet and an equally red tail. The creature turned toward Leo and growled low in her throat.

Sarah recognized the big cat from earlier, in the valley.

Leo's hand tightened in hers.

"Stay calm," said Leo's grandfather. "Take care of her now."

The other Leo concentrated, and then frowned. "It didn't work!" He shook the tube.

The monstrous cat snarled and took a step toward him.

He froze. "What do I do?"

"Try again," said his grandfather.

Again, Leo aimed. But again, nothing happened.

The tube trembled in his hands as the cat took another step toward him.

Sarah's own heart pounded faster. If she didn't know that Leo was safe beside her, she would think she was about to see the boy's demise.

Crack!

Sarah jumped at the sound as the cat bolted, disappearing into the woods. Leo's grandfather held a stick that he had smacked against a nearby tree.

Leo dropped the white tube. He ran to his grandfather and threw his arms around the man's middle. "I'm so sorry."

"Not your fault." His grandfather patted his head. "Nothing we can do now."

"What if it comes back?" asked Leo.

"I'll scare it off again." His grandfather ruffled his hair.

Sarah waited for Leo to do something, but he dropped her hand. They were back in the bamboo, the sounds of the rhinocorn finally beginning to fade into the distance.

Sarah studied Leo as he simply stared at the sand.

She wanted to know what happened, even if that something was awful. "What happened after that?"

"I don't want to know," said Nacho.

Marco shook his head. "Me neither."

"But it's necessary for you to know." Leo sighed heavily. "I'm not sure you all believe how much I need your help. Seeing will be—"

"Believing?" asked Marco.

Leo nodded.

"Wait." Nacho held up a hand. "Someone needs to explain why the old guy"—he pointed at Leo—"and you, had gills."

Marco said, "Leo, you don't have to keep pretending for us. You can be yourself." He met Sarah's gaze. "Right?"

As much as Sarah was freaked by Leo's true appearance, the boy shouldn't have to pretend to look human, just because he thought it made them more comfortable. So she nodded. "You are who you are. That won't change just because you look different."

Leo faced Nacho. "Please don't—"

"Freak out?" Marco grinned.

Leo nodded.

Nacho's forehead creased.

Leo's face slowly changed. Gills appeared as his ears

77

decreased to small holes on the sides of his head. He held up his hands and spread out his fingers, revealing webs between them.

Nacho's eyes grew large and he whispered, "Aquatic apes."

Leo frowned. "What?"

"Never mind." Nacho shook his head. "As long as you don't try to freeze me again, I can deal with this." He shrugged. "It's pretty cool actually."

Leo smiled a little.

"Show us the rest?" Sarah didn't really want to see what happened, but not knowing was worse.

Leo held up his hands. "Ready?"

Sarah held her hand out to Leo. He took it in his webbed one and squeezed.

But Marco and Nacho just looked at each other.

Sarah rolled her eyes. "Babies."

Nacho took Sarah's hand, then Marco's. "It's okay."

"Fine." Marco reached out for Leo.

Sarah took a deep breath as they closed the circle again. She hoped she wouldn't regret coming along for the ride.

10

They were back in the clearing by the cabin. Marco shivered at the sight of it. The odd squirrel ran past the four of them, darting deeper into the trees. Then Leo on the porch called out, "Dinner!"

The bald man grinned, causing the gills on his face to flutter slightly. "Will I like it?"

The boy laughed. "It's the same as the last meal and you liked that."

Marco felt Leo shift uncomfortably beside him as the memory played out. The boy's grandfather said, "Here, take this." He held out the blurred object.

Leo held it firmly in his arms.

His grandfather said, "I want to pick a little fruit. Unless you already made dessert?"

Leo shrugged. "Dinner was hard enough."

A sudden rustle in the brush on the other side of the clearing caused the old man to halt. The boy on the steps turned back.

A flash of black fur rushed past Marco.

Leo's grandfather whirled about to face the trees, and then froze. The panther with the red tail screamed, then pounced on the old man and knocked him to the ground.

Marco cringed.

Leo's hand tightened around his so hard it hurt.

The cat pinned Leo's grandfather and bared her fangs. Then she lowered her head and began to—

"No!" Sarah cried.

Leo dropped their hands.

Marco was back in the bamboo, cross-legged, sweating. His hands shook at what he'd just seen. No wonder Leo had run from the cabin without stopping to take the perfume bottle. Or anything else.

Sarah covered her face and peeked out through her fingers.

Marco touched Leo's knee. "We'll do whatever we have to. But we'll get you back to your family."

"You mean what's left of it," said Leo quietly.

Marco didn't want to say it, but yes, that's what he

meant. His eyes went to Nacho, then over to Sarah. At least, technically, he still had everyone he'd arrived with. Leo couldn't say the same.

Sarah stood up.

Marco grabbed her arm and tried to yank her back down. "We don't know if that thing is still around!"

Sarah pulled away. She snatched the white tube and then pushed through the bamboo, Ahab at her heels.

The other three followed. Marco said, "Careful!"

Sarah turned. "It's gone. And we need a plan."

"A plan for what?" asked Nacho.

Sarah scowled. "Oh, I don't know. Maybe a plan to get my dad unfrozen and get us OFF THIS STUPID ISLAND before one of us gets eaten!"

Leo frowned.

Sarah quickly said, "Sorry."

Marco swallowed. As soon as they got back to their camp on the beach, Leo would know they didn't have the progenitor. And then what?

Nacho said, "I want to go back to Mom."

Marco knew he couldn't stall. Plus, he wanted to get back to their camp as much as Nacho did. He'd have to deal with Leo when they got there; there would be no more putting it off. He'd come up with something. He reached out for the weapon. "Sarah, I'll take that back."

"Oh, right. And one more thing." Before anyone could stop her, she ran down to the beach and flung the white tube into the waves.

"Hey!" yelled Marco. "We needed that."

Sarah brushed her hands together. "No we didn't. Let's go." Sarah set off, Ahab trotting beside her.

"Stupid." Marco kicked at the sand. He yelled after her, "Why would you do that?"

Sarah turned to face him, walking backward. "Because when you had it, you were in charge. When Leo had it, he was in charge. We're supposed to all be working *together*, so now nobody can be in charge!" She whirled around and kept walking.

Leo and Nacho fell in behind her and the dog.

Marco shook his head and stared out at the water. The tube had sunk beneath the waves. Even if he found it without getting eaten by anything, there was no guarantee it would work.

Maybe Sarah was right. When he held the weapon, he was in charge. But only because he held the weapon. Not because he knew the most or had the best plan. Maybe this would turn out better if they had to rely on something other than a weapon's threat.

He ran to catch up to the others.

The four walked at a brisk pace along the water's

edge. Nacho wandered closer to the waves, but Marco pulled on his shirt to bring him farther up the beach. He was worried about the sharkodile making a return appearance.

Not long after that, Marco recognized the curve before their beach.

"Come on!" Sarah began to run.

The others followed. They turned the corner.

Cashmere Bouchard sat near the waves, staring out toward the horizon. Ahab ran to her and licked her face. The girl appeared to startle, then she put her arms around him.

Sarah reached Cash first and stopped to catch her breath as the others caught up.

Marco was sweaty, his throat dry and parched. The hot day was taking its toll.

Cash's hazel eyes widened, but didn't seem to focus. "Who's there?"

Sarah's hands went to her hips. "Who do you think?"

Cash made no move to get up, but she reached out an arm. "I need help."

Marco stepped closer. A book he'd pulled off the *Moonflight* lay in the sand beside her. The pages of *Lost Treasures of the World* flapped in the breeze. He picked it up.

Cash's eyes still stared straight ahead. "I think something's wrong with me."

Sarah dropped to her knees in the sand. "Are you sick?"

Cash shook her head. "I was sitting here, reading, and then . . ."

"What happened?" Marco sunk to the sand on the other side of her, as Nacho stood by his side.

Cash turned her face in their direction, but her eyes remained unfocused. "The lights went out."

Leo took one slow step back from the group.

Marco started to ask Cash what she meant, but then, instead, he waved a hand in front of her face. No reaction.

Cash had gone blind.

11

Sarah gulped. What were they going to do now that one of them couldn't even see?

Nacho asked, "Does it hurt?"

Cash shook her head. "I just can't see."

Leo cowered behind Nacho.

Marco noticed. "Leo! Do you know anything about this?"

"Who's Leo?" asked Cash.

Nacho said, "He's with us."

Leo took a step back, but Marco grabbed his arm. "Did you do this to her?"

Cash frowned. *"Who's Leo?"*

Nacho said, "The Curator."

Cash's mouth fell open for moment, then she spat out, "What's he doing here?"

Leo glanced up at Marco. "I told you that I didn't know what the atmosphere of my ship would do to humans . . ."

Sarah tried to make sense of it all. "So she's blind forever?!"

"What?" Cash started to cry and tried to get to her feet, but she stumbled and fell.

Sarah helped her up.

Leo said, "No, not forever. Just for a while. I think."

"You *think*?" Cash lunged toward his voice.

Leo stepped back out of her reach. Sarah grabbed Cash's arm. "Listen! He may be our only hope."

"Are you kidding me?" Cash yanked her arm back in a huff and stood there, looking wobbly on her feet.

Nacho asked Leo, "Are you sure it's temporary?"

Leo nodded. "Fairly sure."

"What am I supposed to do until then?" yelled Cash. "I'm blind and it's your fault!"

Ahab barked, obviously impatient with all the yelling.

Sarah set a hand on his head. "Cash, we'll stay with you. It'll be okay. The good thing is that we totally believe everything you told us."

"Oh, *now* you believe me." Cash plopped to the

sand and hugged her knees to her chest. Sarah felt bad that they'd doubted her, but she felt worse that they couldn't do anything to help her. But getting mad at Leo wasn't going to make things better. Or help them free her father.

Marco turned to Leo. "Maybe if you showed her everything you showed us—"

"I can't see!" said Cash. "How can he show me anything?"

As if to answer, Leo sank to the sand beside her and took her hand.

Nacho asked, "Hey. Where's Mom?"

Marco sprinted toward the trees, Nacho and Sarah and Ahab at his heels. They arrived at the camp to find Yvonna curled up on her side on a blanket from the *Moonflight*.

Marco realized he still held the book and tossed it aside as he knelt beside her. "Mom?"

Yvonna reached out and grasped Marco's hand. "Did you find them?"

"I'm here." Nacho knelt on her other side.

Their mom attempted a smile. "I was worried. Where's John?"

Sarah crouched beside them. Ahab shoved his head under her arm, and she hugged him.

Marco's gaze flicked to her, then back to his mom. "He'll . . . be here later."

Sarah's eyes widened, but Marco didn't look at her again. Why was he being evasive? Why didn't he just tell her the truth? But she didn't have any more time to wonder, because Yvonna winced. "Help me up, quick."

Marco and Nacho each took an arm and pulled her to her feet. Yvonna took a few rapid, shaky steps, then dropped to her knees and heaved into the bushes.

Sarah stood up and turned away. Her stepmother couldn't possibly still be seasick, could she? Even food poisoning should have run its course by now, she was pretty sure. She glanced back at them.

Marco bent over his mom and rubbed her back, murmuring something. Suddenly, hot tears stung Sarah's eyes and she whirled around, moving a few steps away. At the moment, she didn't have a mother *or* a father. And she really could have used one, just then. Not a stepmother who was barfing everywhere. She leaned down to pet Ahab. "At least I have you."

Yvonna called, "Sarah?"

Sarah swung around.

Yvonna was back on her feet, leaning on Marco and Nacho. Yvonna held out a hand to Sarah. "Sweetie, are you okay?"

Sarah closed the gap in seconds and flung her arms around her stepmother's waist. "Don't die!"

Yvonna's arms circled Sarah, one hand slipping up to stroke her hair. She chuckled slightly. "That's not going to happen."

Sarah wanted to say so much. How she'd seen her own mom get sick, throwing up much of the time. She didn't see how Yvonna could possibly know she wouldn't die. "But what's wrong with you?" She stepped back, wiping tears from her face with one hand.

Marco took his mom's arm. "You should sit back down."

He and Nacho led her back to the blanket, and when she was once again lying down, she looked from Sarah to Marco to Nacho. "I promise, I'm not dying. I've had this before." She shrugged a bit. "Twice, in fact."

Nacho asked, "And you got better?"

Yvonna laughed weakly. She rubbed Nacho's hair and took Sarah's hand. "You three are going to have a little brother or sister."

Sarah jerked back her hand.

Marco's eyes widened. "What?"

Sarah had no words. Seriously? They were ship-wrecked, a misguided amphibious alien freeze-dried her dad, and now her stepmother was pregnant? Her knees buckled and she dropped to the sand. Ahab plopped down beside her.

Yvonna covered her mouth. Marco grabbed her arm and pulled her up. She barely made it to the bushes before getting sick again.

When she finished, Sarah asked, "So it's morning sickness?"

Yvonna sat back down. "More like all day long. With Nacho, I—" She stopped.

Nacho frowned. "What did I do?"

"Oh, sweetie, nothing. It wasn't your fault." His mom said, "I ended up dehydrated and had to go to the hospital." She quickly shook her head. "That won't happen though."

Sarah stopped her own train of selfish thoughts. She got to her feet, found the nearest bottle of water, and took it to her stepmother. She wasn't thrilled by the idea of a baby, but did not relish the thought of being without yet another adult. As much as she didn't want to admit it, they—she—needed Yvonna. "You should drink."

Yvonna nodded. "I've been trying."

"What did they do in the hospital?" Marco's forehead wrinkled, his lips drawn downward.

Sarah realized he was really worried about his mom.

"They gave me IVs." Yvonna held up the bottle of water. "This will have to do."

"We have to get off this island." Sarah met Marco's gaze. "But first we have to tell you about Dad." She scooted closer to Yvonna. Marco sat next to his mom, who reached out and squeezed his knee.

Marco said, "We found the cave. The one that Cash told us about."

"Where is Cash?" asked his mom.

"Down on the beach. But, Mom, everything she told us was true."

"Except that it wasn't exactly a cave. Not like the one we all slept in," said Sarah.

Yvonna frowned. "What exactly was it?" She glanced the way they'd come. "And, Sarah, when's your dad coming?"

Sarah chewed on the inside of her lip. She had a feeling her stepmother was not going to believe them.

Marco cleared his throat. "It was sort of a space-ship."

Yvonna rolled her eyes. "Okay. Fine." She called out weakly, "John! Very funny. You can come out now."

Sarah said, "We're serious."

Yvonna shook her head. "I know you're trying to pass the time and have some fun, but I really feel lousy and I just need John to be here right now." She clapped her hand over her mouth and tried to stand up, but collapsed on her side instead and vomited in the sand beside the blanket.

Sarah quickly stood and walked away, Ahab beside her. But the retching sounds followed. As did the worry about how they were going to go about finding help for Yvonna. And of course, the biggest worry of all: Would they ever get themselves off the island? She needed her dad and she needed him now. And she would do whatever it took to get him back as soon as possible.

12

Marco stayed with his mom until she was asleep, then went to check on the others. Nacho had gone back to the beach to check on Cash and Leo, and from what he could see, his brother and the other two seemed to be getting along. He noticed Sarah, sitting with Ahab under one of the monkey pod trees.

He walked over to her. "My mom's asleep."

Sarah gazed up at him. "We need to get my dad and we need to get off this island."

Marco nodded. "I know. I guess telling her the truth about your dad didn't help much."

Sarah shook her head. "Doesn't matter. She's too sick to help anyway."

Marco chuckled a little.

Sarah frowned. "It's funny that she's sick?"

"No." Marco dropped to the ground and sat cross-legged. He rubbed Ahab's neck. "A baby. That's kind of funny."

"I don't think it's funny." Sarah scowled. "I don't think any of this is funny."

All this time Marco had it in the back of his mind that Sarah and John were temporary. If they could survive this trip, get back home, then his mom would admit the whole thing was a mistake. The shipwreck of a trip was an exclamation point to the disaster of a marriage.

But . . . a baby? A baby was the opposite of temporary.

Marco laughed then, a real laugh.

Sarah raised her eyebrows at him.

He gasped through his laughter, "Don't you get it? I thought this whole mess would tear them apart."

The corners of Sarah's mouth turned up. "I thought we'd get back and never have to see each other again."

Marco laughed. "But now. A baby."

"I'm never getting rid of you." Sarah laughed. "You know what else totally isn't funny?"

"What?" Marco could barely get the word out.

Sarah bent over, laughing, then finally spit out,

"What happens when Leo finds out we don't have his progenitor?" She took a gasping breath. "How will we get my dad out then?"

Marco laughed more. "What if a boat never comes? And we have to live here forever?"

They laughed, neither able to get another word out. Ahab's tail wagged.

Finally, Sarah giggled one more time, then slashed her hand across her neck. "Okay. Done now." She sighed and set a hand on Ahab's head. "But seriously. What will we do when Leo finds out?"

Marco swallowed. He hadn't really wanted to ask that question; he was afraid of what the answer would be. "We'll have to trick him, somehow." He glanced at his mom, who was still sleeping. "I guess we sit here and figure it out."

Sarah pointed. "What's that?"

Marco swiveled in the direction she was pointing. The book he'd carried up from the beach lay in the sand. "Oh, I pulled it off the *Moonflight*. Cash had it."

Sarah retrieved the book, then plopped back down and started to page through it. Ahab pushed his nose into it, and she gently shoved him aside. "Have you read it?" Then she rolled her eyes. "Oh, right. Dumb question. You don't read."

"I read." Marco frowned. "I read your Harry Potter on the plane."

She raised her eyebrows. "You did?"

He nodded.

She frowned a little. "Why didn't you tell me before?"

"I didn't want you to be right." Marco shrugged. "Or I guess I didn't want to give you the satisfaction of being right."

She grinned. "So you liked it?"

"Yeah. But I didn't want you to know that . . ." He stopped, unsure he trusted her enough to tell her.

"What?"

"I've never been a big reader, but not because I don't like the stories. Reading has always been hard for me." He swallowed. "It's better than it used to be. It helps if the book is really interesting."

Sarah sucked on her lower lip for a moment. "I'm sorry that I made such a big deal about you not reading Harry Potter before."

"Doesn't matter." Marco smiled. "I plan on borrowing the rest when we get back home. But then you have to watch the movies with me."

"It's a deal." Sarah dropped her head back down

to read. "So this is actually kind of cool. All these treasures that are supposed to exist, but the people who lost them are the only ones who seem to have ever seen them."

"Like what kind of treasures?" asked Marco.

Sarah set a finger on a page. "Well, like the Ark of the Covenant from the Bible for one."

"Like in that old Indiana Jones movie?" asked Marco.

Sarah nodded. "But it's supposed to be real. And it's in Ethiopia."

Marco had had enough of having to believe things that seemed impossible. He was done for the day. He dropped to his side and rested his head on his arm. He yawned and shut his eyes as he heard another page turn.

Sarah said, "Here's another one. Some samurai sword that is supposed to be magic."

Another page flipped.

Marco was so tired he began to doze off.

Sarah kept talking. "Here's a tribe that claims they were visited by aliens. The aliens gave them a gift, but treasure hunters stole it and it's never been seen again. . . ."

Silence. No more pages.

"Marco."

He sighed. "What?"

"Get this. The tribe says the aliens were mermaids—and mermen."

Marco's eyes snapped open. "Did you say mermaids?"

Sarah pointed. "Does that look familiar to you?"

Marco sat up and grabbed the book from Sarah. A black-and-white drawing filled the two-page spread. A wooden box, with intricate drawings and ancient lettering. Lettering he had seen before.

His eyes locked with Sarah's. She quickly jumped up and ran over to the chest from the *Moonflight*. She yanked the towel off just as Marco got there, Ahab panting at his side.

His heart began to pound. "Oh, *wow*."

The two stood there, gazes shifting between the drawing and the chest.

They were the same.

Marco hesitated. Or did he only *wish* they were the same? He asked Sarah, "It's the same, right?"

"It's *definitely* the same." Sarah had a funny look on her face. "I think Cash saw it before. I think this is what the bad guy on her boat was looking for. He, or someone else, stole it from the tribe in Africa and brought it here. He had to leave it when he was rescued. But then he didn't recognize the island because of what Leo and his grandfather did."

Marco swallowed. "Do you know what this means?"

Sarah smiled. "You weren't lying to Leo at all. This is the other half of the progenitor. Leo can make what he needs to fill the containers and *let my dad go!*"

13

Sarah grabbed Marco's arm. "We have to show Leo."

"I'll go get them." Marco ran off toward the others.

Sarah grinned and hugged Ahab as her head swam with possibilities. "We can get my dad out!" Then they could help Leo fill the containers. Then maybe he could use the progenitor to make them a boat and they could all go home.

Nacho and Leo jogged toward her, as Marco slowly led Cash behind them. Sarah asked her, "Are you okay?"

Cash shrugged. "I'm a little freaked out right now after what he showed me."

Nacho asked, "You could see?"

Cash nodded. "Like it was a dream or something, inside my head. And—"

"What?" asked Sarah.

"I understand a little bit why he did it," said Cash. "But I'm still mad."

Leo looked uncomfortable.

Sarah told him, "We have something for you." She stepped aside.

Leo's eyes narrowed as he leaned forward and ran his fingers over the carved symbols on the chest. "This is my language."

"Is it the progenitor?" asked Marco.

"I don't know." Leo dropped to his knees beside the chest, peering closely. He rested one webbed hand on the top. "We must open it."

Marco said, "I tried before. No luck."

Leo's lips moved slightly as he looked at the words.

Sarah whispered, "Is he reading it?"

Leo looked up at her. "I can hear you."

Sarah shrugged. "Sorry, just wondered."

"What's happening?" asked Cash.

Sarah said, "The chest from the boat. We think it might be what Leo's looking for."

Leo said, "It's my language, but an earlier version of it. It's not easy."

"Do you know what it says?" asked Nacho.

Leo shook his head. "Not yet. I think the words might be some kind of directions."

"Directions to what?" asked Marco.

"Directions on how to open it." Leo went back to running his fingers over the carvings.

Nacho said, "Maybe we should leave him alone." He took Cash's elbow. "Let's go see how the fire is."

"I think I let it go out," said Cash.

"Then I'll build us a new one," said Nacho.

Marco said, "I'm going to check on my mom."

Sarah and Ahab followed him the short distance to where Yvonna lay on the blanket.

Marco knelt beside her. "Mom?"

Her eyes opened and she smiled. "Help me sit up?"

Sarah went to her other side and held her elbow. They pulled until she was upright. Yvonna hugged her knees and set her head sideways on them. "Is John back yet?"

"No," said Marco.

Since hearing about the baby, Sarah had been thinking so many things. For one, it was like Marco said, they could no longer expect they would be going their separate ways. A baby was something that brought families together, not split them apart. And if Yvonna was only after her dad's money, she wouldn't be happy about having a baby.

Sarah had to admit that maybe she was wrong about Yvonna. Maybe her dad had found someone to love who truly loved him back.

Sarah didn't want to worry Yvonna about her dad until they had to. So she said, "He'll be back soon." She picked up the bottle of water that lay beside her. "A drink?"

Yvonna nodded and took a swig from the bottle. Her hair was damp, loose tendrils of it stuck down around her glistening, sweaty face. "I'm so hot."

Marco asked, "Do you want to go in the water?"

Sarah shook her head and widened her eyes at him. They couldn't let her go in the water, not without knowing where that sharkodile was. "I could bring you some. To soak your feet in." Of course, that meant she had to go in the water. But she would do it.

Yvonna shook her head. "No. I think I just want to lie down again."

"Are you feeling any better?" asked Marco.

Sarah hoped she would say yes.

Instead, her stepmother set a hand on her forehead.

"I'm so dizzy." Marco quickly helped her lie down. By the time she fell asleep, Sarah realized they would have to add getting help for her to the list of everything else on their list of impossible tasks.

Marco whispered, "She's not getting better. She needs an IV or some kind of hydration she can keep down."

Nacho came over. "Leo thinks he figured out how to open the chest."

Sarah exchanged a glance with Marco. She hoped that the progenitor was in the chest so that she could get her dad back. And then, perhaps, they could escape the island and get help for Yvonna.

Marco trudged over to the chest.

Sarah wondered why he wasn't more excited. If, as they all hoped, the progenitor was truly in there, then Leo could get home. And, before he left, he would set her dad free.

All good things, in her opinion. But maybe Marco was just really worried about his mom.

Sarah hoped there was something in that chest to be able to help Yvonna. She told Leo, "Go ahead. Open it!"

Leo looked around at all of them. "I need you to look away."

"Why?" asked Nacho.

Leo didn't answer at first.

"I feel like you're not telling us something," said Marco.

Leo shrugged. "I don't actually know if you can look at it or not. I just blurred it in the memory in case it would harm you in some way."

He *had* been protecting them. They hadn't given him a lot of reason to trust them, yet he truly seemed to be concerned for their well-being. Sarah reached out and touched his arm. "Thanks. For caring about us."

Leo said, "So, maybe you all should turn away. Until I see what's in here."

Marco crossed his arms and looked into the distance.

Cash said, "What I don't get is how this chest, if it is what Leo needs, ended up on this island?"

Marco said, "I hauled it off the *Moonflight*. I don't know where the captain got it."

Sarah blurted out, "Leo!"

Leo stopped what he was doing.

She said, "You said you traced the other half of the progenitor here, right?"

He nodded. "But it wasn't here." He set a hand on the chest. "This was not on the island."

Sarah looked over at Marco. "Captain Norm had

been to this island before. We found Ahab's tags, so we *know* he was here before. What if this chest was here and he took it?"

Marco shook his head. "But how did it get here? Someone would have had to steal it and bring it here."

Sarah said, "According to the book, a lot of those treasures get stolen and sold within a few days. The thieves only want the money they can get for the treasure most of the time."

Marco said, "So someone could have bought it from the thieves and transported it."

Leo said, "But why would they leave it here? When someone else could just take it and—"

Sarah asked, "Cash, you've seen the chest before, haven't you?"

Cash shook her head. "I never saw it." She was quiet a moment before adding, "But I overheard it described. By Fox."

Sarah sucked in a breath and glanced at Marco.

"I'm sorry I didn't tell y'all before. I . . . I wasn't sure I trusted everyone." Cash shrugged. Marco and Sarah exchanged a glance. Maybe it was time for them to trust Cash all the way. Marco said, "We think this might be the island Fox wanted to find."

Cash asked, "What makes you say that?"

Sarah said, "We saw a face rock earlier."

Cash slowly dropped to her knees. "This is the island?"

"I think so." Marco said, "When Fox was here, it wouldn't have been much but sand and rocks."

Leo said, "No one would recognize it from even one of your years past."

Sarah gazed at the chest. "So this has to be the treasure Fox is looking for." Her eyes rose to meet Marco's.

Cash said, "Makes sense to me."

"What does that mean? Who is Fox?" asked Leo.

Sarah smiled. "It means they'll be back. And we'll have a way out of here." She told Leo, "Let's open it and then go get my dad."

14

Leo stood in front of the chest. "I still think you should all turn around, just in case. Okay?"

Sarah said, "We'll just watch until you're gonna open it."

"Yeah," said Marco.

Leo frowned. "All right. But you must do what I say."

Cash stayed in the sand where she was. "Can you tell me what's happening?"

Nacho, Sarah, and Marco all crept in closer. Sarah grabbed Ahab's collar.

Leo spread his fingers, which made the webbing even more apparent, and set them on top of the chest. He then slid one hand to the left and the other to the right, inching toward the lower corners of the chest. He paused. His chest rose up, as if to take a large breath. Then his hands pushed down, so very hard that his chin wobbled with the effort.

Mist rose around, shrouding him.

Marco nudged both Sarah and Nacho back a couple of steps. Ahab bumped Cash, who asked, "What's going on?"

"Nothing. Yet." Marco's breath caught in his throat as the mist continued to thicken and rise, until the chest and Leo were enveloped, nearly invisible. His heart sped up.

"Is it opening?" asked Cash.

Marco said, "I don't know—"

Suddenly, a light shot out of the mist, straight up, and Leo cried out.

"What happened?" cried Cash.

Marco held his breath.

The light vanished.

Slowly, the mist dissipated.

The top of the chest was raised, blocking their view of Leo.

Sarah stepped forward, pulling Ahab, but Marco grabbed her arm. "Don't."

Sarah shook him off and took another step. "Leo? Are you okay?"

"Y'all?" Cash tried to stand up, but Nacho set a hand on her shoulder and whispered, "Leo got it open."

Leo stood up. His face was paler than before, but slowly the color returned. "You found it." The corners of his mouth turned up. "The other half of the progenitor is really here."

Marco moved toward the chest, but Leo held up a hand. "Stop."

"Kids?"

They all turned.

Yvonna walked up behind Leo, wobbling a little. She set a hand on her forehead. "What's going on?"

Leo held out a hand. "Don't come any closer."

Yvonna's eyes widened as she stared at Leo. "What in the—" Her startled gaze went to the chest, and whatever lay inside.

And then she collapsed.

Marco ran and dropped to his knees beside her. "Mom?" He slid an arm under her and lifted up her torso. He gently patted her face. *"Mom!"* She didn't respond. Marco didn't know what to think. Did she collapse because she was sick? Or because of what she saw in the chest?

Slam!

Leo shut the chest. "I'm so sorry."

Marco's hands trembled. To have something terrible happen to his mom, the way Cash's time as Leo's prisoner had made her blind, terrified him. "We need to get help."

Nacho turned to Leo. "Can't you do anything? Don't you have some kind of medicine?"

Leo nodded. "But I don't know if I can help her."

Sarah said, "You have to try."

Leo hesitated. "But I—"

Sarah pointed at Yvonna. "My stepmom is sick. Really sick. If you can help her, you have to."

Leo said, "But I'm running out of time. Now that I have the whole progenitor, I can finish what my grandfather started. And I can leave here."

Marco's heart pounded harder. "We had a deal! You have to let my stepdad go and then you have to help my mom."

Leo's voice was shaky as he said, "I don't know if I can."

Sarah let go of Ahab, pushed past Leo, and sat down on the chest. "Then *I don't know* if you can have the chest."

Marco darted a look at her. What was she doing?

Leo stood up straighter. "But I already do."

Nacho sat next to Sarah. "Seems to me like we have the chest."

Leo frowned. "But you gave it to me."

"Well, we're taking it back," said Sarah. "You said you'd unfreeze my dad."

"What if I help you?" asked Leo.

Sarah folded her arms. "That would be a start."

Leo began to pace. "I don't know if our medicine will work on humans."

Marco said, "She's pregnant. I think she's just dehydrated. I mean, unless the thing in that chest did something to her, she just needs fluids. Like an IV of some kind. You must have something like that?"

"Perhaps." Leo nodded. "If you help me take the chest to my ship, then I can give you the medicine."

Sarah frowned. "Wait just a second. You made a deal. We proved we have what you want; now you give us what we want. You let my dad go and then you can have the chest."

Leo's eyes narrowed. "But I need to take the chest now. So I can get started."

Sarah glanced at Marco.

He wasn't sure what her plan was, but he gave her a nod to let her know he was on board, whatever it was.

She held up a finger. "You thaw my dad out." Another finger snapped up. "You give us medicine. Then you get your chest."

"What about me?" asked Cash.

Sarah popped up another finger. "You make Cash see again."

Leo put both hands over his face.

"You're wasting time," said Marco. "You know you're not getting the chest until you help us first." He looked down at his mom. "She needs help now."

"Fine." Leo began to walk away.

Marco called out, "Hold up! You're not going alone." Marco gently lowered his mom to the sand and stood up.

Leo whirled around to face Marco. "If you want the medicine, I need to go back to the cavern, my ship."

"Where you can get another tube, or maybe a weapon we don't even know about." Marco shook his head. "I'm not stupid." He pointed at the chest. "If you get what you want, then we will never get what we need."

Leo said, "But I do need the chest. You know I do. Don't you trust me by now?"

"Um, Marco?" Nacho slid off the chest.

Marco ignored his brother. "I know what you've told

113

us and shown us. But *trust* you?" He shook his head. "I don't know. And I'm not willing to take a chance." He pointed at his mom. "It's not worth the risk."

Leo asked, "So what do you suggest?"

Sarah hopped off the chest. "I'll go with you."

"Marco!" yelled Nacho.

The three turned to look at him.

Nacho's right arm was extended behind him, pointing toward the water. "Look."

Marco's gaze went out to the lagoon. And immediately focused on the sailboat entering the far end of it, still so small he could just make out the white sails.

Sarah screeched. "We're saved!" She waved her arms and sprinted down the sand. "Help!"

Ahab barked and followed her.

"Is it a boat?" asked Cash.

Marco took a step to follow, then froze. He asked Cash, "What does your grandfather's boat look like?"

Cash said, "White sails, white hull. HMS *Cashmere* painted on the side. Is it Sarge? Are they here?"

"Wait a sec." Marco ran over to the pile of things off the *Moonflight* and found what he was looking for. Binoculars. He raised them to his eyes and aimed toward the boat with white sails and a white hull. "One man at the wheel. Another beside him." He lowered the binoculars to the hull. "HMS *Cashmere.*"

"It's them!" cried Cash, a huge smile on her face.

Sarah and Ahab had reached the water's edge.

Leo asked, "Who are the people on the boat?"

Cash said, "My grandfather. And two people with a gun, looking for their treasure. Your chest, if our theory is right."

Marco glanced at the chest. "Do you think Fox figured out that this is the island?"

Cash shook her head. "It looks so different and he never even thought about looking for the face rock here. Maybe they gave up and just came back to get me?"

Nacho said, "They can give us a ride back."

"I doubt it. They basically boat-jacked Cash's grandpa. They won't want any more witnesses than they already have." Marco scratched his head and tried to figure out what they should do.

"What if they use the gun to take the chest?" asked Leo.

Marco swallowed. "We can't let that happen." He cupped his hands around his mouth. "Sarah!"

She didn't turn around.

So he tried again, "Sarah!"

Finally she turned, waving and jumping up and down.

He beckoned with an arm.

She raised both her arms in the air.

He beckoned again.

She dropped her arms, shook her head, and then jogged toward them, Ahab beside her, tail wagging, tongue flopping. "What? I wanted to make sure they didn't leave without us."

Marco said, "It's Cash's grandpa's boat. With the people looking for the treasure."

Sarah's eyes widened. "Do they know this is the island?"

Cash said, "We don't know. But we can't let them get the chest or they'll leave us all here."

"What do we do?" asked Sarah.

Marco glanced at Leo. "Leo and I will take the chest to his cavern. We can't risk Fox getting it. Sarah, we'll get your dad out, and then we'll come back." He took ahold of Sarah's arm. "You need to stay here with Nacho and Cash and take care of my mom."

"Why can't I go with Leo?" asked Sarah.

Marco pointed at the beach. "Because if they had binoculars, they already saw you. You stay here, make up some story about how you and my mom and Nacho were the only survivors of a shipwreck or something."

Sarah shook her head. "I don't want to, I—"

Marco forced his voice to be gentle. "You can do it. You have to. You have to let them think it's only the three of you with Cash. My mom's sick, Cash is blind, Nacho's just a kid—"

"I'm standing right here, you know." Nacho frowned.

Marco rolled his eyes. "And you're just a girl—"

"Hey!" Sarah protested.

"Listen. I didn't mean it like it sounded. To a guy with a gun, a skinny girl is no threat to him. And we need him to think you're no threat, okay?" Marco held his breath, hoping she'd go along with it.

Sarah nodded. "Okay."

"We have to go because it'll be dark soon," said Marco.

"Maybe they won't come ashore until tomorrow," said Cash.

"I can't take that chance," said Marco. "We need to go now." He hugged Nacho and then told Sarah, "Please take care of my mom." He gave Ahab a quick pat on the head, then knelt beside his mom, kissed her on the cheek, and then laid a hand on her forehead. "I'll be back." Then he got to his feet and grabbed one side of the chest. He looked across to the other end where Leo stood, looking at him.

"What?" asked Marco.

"You can trust me. I swear," said Leo.

"I'm counting on it." He glanced at his mom, then the others. "We're all counting on it. On three. One, two, three." Together they lifted the chest. Marco adjusted his hands.

The thing wasn't that heavy, but holding it was awkward. The trip would take them a while because they'd have to stop along the way to rest. He told Sarah, "You guys have to stall them, okay? Do *not* get on that boat."

"I don't plan on it," said Sarah.

Marco nodded. "Whatever you have to say, do it. We'll get back here as soon as we can."

Nacho and Sarah looked at each other. "We're good," said Sarah.

Marco told Leo, "Let's go." With the chest between the two of them, they headed off through the trees.

Sarah called after them, "Good luck."

Marco glanced back at her. She seemed like she was trying to be brave, but he could tell she was scared. "You too." He hated to leave them, especially his mom. How would they deal with a man with a gun?

But his best chance was to free John. His stepdad would know what to do. Marco hoped so anyway.

They hurried, carrying the chest between them, ducking under tree branches and swerving to avoid obstacles on the ground. Marco realized something else—after everything that happened, he had come to actually like Sarah. She still annoyed him half the time, but she certainly wasn't the stupid, self-centered girl he thought she was. He was okay with having her around.

Walking away and leaving her behind felt strange. Because quite honestly, she was part of his family now, and he did not want anything to happen to her. He hoped nothing did.

15

Sarah's stomach clenched as she watched Marco walk away. She never thought she'd be unhappy to see him leave, but as he disappeared with Leo and the chest, she felt tears well up in her eyes. How was she going to do this without him?

"You okay?" asked Nacho.

Sarah nodded and quickly swiped away the tear that spilled over and ran down her cheek. "Yeah. Just kinda worried."

Cash called out, "But Sarge is here. Or at least out there. He won't let anything happen to me. Or you guys." She tilted her head. "Or your mom."

Sarah wondered how Cash could promise that. Sarge hadn't exactly been able to stop Fox from stranding Cash, had he? Sarah dropped to the sand and touched her stepmom's shoulder lightly. "Yvonna?"

Yvonna's eyelids fluttered a little. She moaned and set a hand over her eyes. "It's so bright."

Sarah's dark eyes met Nacho's. Was he thinking the same thing? Wondering if whatever was in the chest had done some kind of damage to Yvonna?

Sarah felt a slight chill and looked up. The sun had gone down far enough so that the shade extended far beyond their camp. "It'll be dark soon." She hadn't spent a night alone. Well, she hadn't spent a night without an alert and capable adult. And there was no way they would make it to the cave they'd stayed in the night before. She looked overhead to the platform and the mattresses. "We've got to get her up there."

"No way. We'll never be able to." Nacho shot a look at the fire, which had dwindled to a weak stream of smoke. "I can build up the fire some more. We could stay there."

Sarah thought of the crabs. "We need to be up in the trees."

Nacho glanced overhead. "But we can't leave my mom down here alone."

Sarah sighed. "I know." She took Cash's elbow. "Let's get you over to the fire."

Together, Sarah and Nacho threw more wood on the fire. The pile seemed bigger than earlier. Sarah asked Cash, "Did you gather wood?"

Cash nodded. "Before the lights went out. I wanted to help."

Sarah smiled. "Well, you did. Nacho, help me get your mom over here."

Sarah grabbed the blanket Yvonna had been lying on and took it over to where her stepmom had collapsed. She spread it out, then Nacho helped her roll Yvonna onto it. They each grabbed hold of a side and began to drag her through the sand.

Sarah's back started to hurt at the strain. "Rest. For just a second." As they caught their breath, they looked out in the lagoon. Dusk was upon them, and lights from the sailboat glittered.

Nacho said, "I thought maybe they'd come in by now."

Sarah said, "I don't think they're coming tonight. Maybe they didn't see me after all."

Nacho pointed at the fire. "Well, they might see that."

Which could be good or bad, Sarah thought, depending on how you looked at it. She would have liked an adult there, even one with a gun, because she had no idea what might happen in the night. She also couldn't help but think about the black cat with the crimson beard and tail, still loose on the island. And probably still hungry.

"Okay. Let's go again," said Nacho.

They took up their edges of the blanket and pulled some more, Ahab trotting beside them, providing moral support. After another rest break and more heaving, they finally arrived at the fire.

Sarah ran back to grab a couple of pillows, then placed them under Yvonna's head. Nacho had several beach towels tucked under one arm, a mesh bag hooked on the other. He dropped the bag and spread out a towel for Cash, then helped her onto it. Once she was comfortable, Nacho plopped down on another towel as Sarah claimed the last one, Ahab joining her.

Nacho pulled a bottle of water out of the bag and handed it to Sarah.

Sarah hadn't realized how thirsty she was until she began drinking. As she downed half of the bottle, her stomach growled and gurgled. She poured some in her hand, and Ahab licked it up.

Nacho handed Cash a granola bar, then tossed two to Sarah. "Thanks." She smiled and ripped off the wrapper, devouring the first bar in less than four bites.

She read the label of the other one and peeled off the wrapper. "Well, boy, I think this is dog friendly." Ahab devoured it and wagged his tail.

Sarah opened another bottle of water and moved closer to Yvonna. She set a hand under her head to tip it up, and then set the bottle on her stepmom's lips. "You need to drink."

Yvonna managed to get a few swallows in before dropping her head back down.

Cash said, "So you're gonna get a brother or sister, huh?"

Sarah locked eyes with Nacho, who grinned.

"Are you happy about that?" Cash asked.

Nacho said, "Yeah. I hope it's a boy."

Sarah didn't answer right away. At first, when Yvonna told them she was pregnant, she'd been shocked. But as she'd thought about it, she warmed to the idea. A little, anyway. She hadn't been around babies very much. She said, "Maybe it won't be that bad."

Cash nodded. "Babies are cool. I have a little cousin who is one. He's really fun." She took a bite of a granola bar.

Neither of them said anything else. Sarah stared into the flames as the night gradually descended around them.

Cash lay down on her side and shut her eyes.

Sarah tried not to think about what might be out there. She picked up a stick and poked it into the fire, stirring up the glowing coals. "Too bad we don't have marshmallows."

Nacho nodded. "Yeah." He yawned.

Sarah said, "You can go to sleep."

"But we should keep watch," said Nacho.

Sarah nodded. "I'll take the first shift."

"Okay," said Nacho. "But make sure to wake me up."

"I will," said Sarah.

Nacho reclined beside the fire and shut his eyes. Within minutes, his breathing slowed and his mouth fell open. How could that boy sleep? Sarah was fairly certain she wouldn't be able to. Her heart pounded too hard.

What if the crabs came back?

What if one of Leo's freaky animals showed up?

She gazed out at the water where the lights of the sailboat glowed in the darkness. She wished those people would have come ashore before dark, even if they were bad. Being the lone one awake and alert made her feel so . . . *responsible.*

Sarah yawned. After everything that happened that day, stressed out or not, she couldn't fight the exhaustion.

She pulled a blanket up over Yvonna. As far as she could tell, her stepmother was asleep. So she went back to her spot by the fire and hunkered down a bit, trying to get more comfortable in the sand herself. Ahab stretched out and fell asleep.

Sarah lay down on her side, head propped up on her elbow as she watched the flickering fire. Maybe she should relish the peace, because who knew what would happen in the morning when the boat-jackers came ashore?

She yawned again. "You have to stay awake."

But she let her eyes shut. Only for a moment. She was simply so tired, and it was so hard to keep them open. She couldn't help it.

"Sarah!"

Cash's panicked voice startled Sarah awake. Immediately, her heart pounded and her hands trembled. The fire was still bright, the night was still dark. Cash's face was illuminated only by the firelight.

"What's wrong?" whispered Sarah.

Cash whispered back, "I heard something. From over there." She pointed toward the trees.

Ahab whined.

Sarah quickly tossed more wood on the fire. Whatever was out there, she hoped it hated fire. The flames

126

might be their best—if not only—defense. For the first time, she wished she hadn't thrown that white tube into the waves. "Do you see anything?" Then she realized how stupid her question was.

They huddled together, Sarah stoking the fire. She set aside a club-sized piece of wood.

Nacho's eyes opened at a crashing in the bushes. He crawled next to Ahab and Sarah. She felt like her heart would pound its way out of her chest.

Nacho leaned into her, his voice so quiet Sarah could barely hear him as he asked, "What do you think it is?"

Sarah didn't want to think about what might be making the sound. "Probably nothing."

She looked sideways at Nacho, who raised his eyebrows at her. Sarah shrugged. "Isn't that better than telling you it might be something that could eat us?"

A corner of his mouth turned up. "Yeah."

Sarah picked up the piece of wood she'd set aside and let the end catch fire, then handed it to Nacho. Nacho stood up. Sarah did the same to another stick and got to her feet.

"Are you going in there?" asked Cash.

"Either that or we stay here, huddled like frightened rabbits all night." Sarah sounded far braver than she felt. "Let's go, boy." Ahab got to his feet beside her.

Nacho nodded. "Let's do it."

Side by side, brandishing their torches, they crept toward the edge of the trees where they'd heard the sound. Sarah tried to hold the torch steady in her shaking hand. Impossible, so she reached up with her other hand, clutching the stick with both. She held it out in front of her.

Suddenly, a ball of fur jumped out at them.

Ahab barked and Sarah screamed as Nacho yelled. Sarah scrunched her eyes shut as she jabbed out with her torch, waiting for something to attack her.

Nacho began to laugh.

Sarah opened her eyes.

Ahab barked again.

The squirrel with the striped tail sat there, nose twitching at them. "It's not funny." But as she looked at the squirrel, then back at Nacho, she realized it was funny. And she began to laugh too, so hard that she had to bend over and clutch her stomach. She dropped the torch, which landed with a fizz in the sand.

Still laughing, Nacho grabbed her arm. "Come on. Let's go back to the fire."

Ahab wanted to keep barking at the creature, so

Sarah pulled him by the collar until he followed them. They sat back down.

Cash asked, "Did you see anything?"

Sarah giggled. "A very weird squirrel."

Nacho said, "Let's just build up the fire and go to sleep. If we get eaten, we get eaten."

"By a squirrel?" asked Cash.

They began to laugh again. Then, finally, Sarah lay down beside Ahab and fell asleep, putting a stop, at last, to what had seemed like a never-ending day.

16

By the time the sun went down, Marco and Leo had stopped to rest exactly four times. Marco estimated the weight of the chest as not more than twenty-five pounds or so, but it was the size of a large suitcase and awkward to carry. They continued to move in the dusk on the flat, sandy beach. Marco kicked something with his foot, and saw a rock roll out of the way. A moment later, he tripped on a piece of driftwood and fell to one knee, letting his end of the chest drop to the sand. He shook his head. "It's getting too dark."

Leo set his end of the chest in the sand. His face was barely visible in the waning light.

Marco said, "I don't know why I didn't think to bring a flashlight." He glanced at the chest. "I guess I couldn't have carried it anyway." Clouds began to cover the moon and stars. Soon they wouldn't have any light to see by. "I can't believe this. We're gonna have to stop for the night."

"Why?" asked Leo.

"Duh. We can't see." Marco rolled his eyes.

Leo said, "Light is not a problem."

Marco mumbled, "No, just the *lack* of it is."

Suddenly a glowing blue bubble of light surrounded them, spreading out about ten yards, revealing the sand and even stretching to the waves slipping up on the sand.

"Whoa!" Marco jumped back, but the light stayed with him.

He ran to the side a few feet. The light followed.

Marco juked and dodged, but couldn't escape the blueness. Finally, he stopped trying. "What is that?"

Leo held out his hands. "Light. So we can keep going."

Marco relaxed. The inside of the bubble was as light as day. Just more . . . *blue.* "How did you do that?"

Leo turned one arm over and slid up his sleeve, revealing the black bracelet from before. "Technology."

Marco grinned. "Can that thing make me a sandwich?"

Leo smiled and shook his head. "That has to wait until we're back at the ship."

Marco leaned down and grabbed his end of the chest. "Well then, let's go."

The light made things so much easier. Other than the brief periodic stops, they made good time along the beach. As they neared the spot where the sharkodile had attacked them, Leo set his end of the chest in the sand.

"Why are you stopping?" asked Marco.

"I need a rest," Leo said.

Marco firmed up his grip. "We need to keep going. We can't stop here."

Leo wiped some sweat off his face. "I have to rest."

Marco dropped his end of the chest. "Listen, this is not a good place." His gaze darted out to the waves, lit by the blue light for a little ways offshore. "Some . . . thing came after us here."

Leo whirled to face the water. "A shark. With feet."

Marco frowned. "Yeah. How did you know?"

Leo shrugged. "One of our mistakes."

Marco sucked on his lower lip for a moment and asked something he wasn't sure he wanted an answer to. "Did you make anything else that went in the water?"

Leo picked up his end of the chest. "I think we should get going."

Marco hefted his end, and they used quick steps for the next several minutes. When Leo finally slowed down, Marco did too. They rounded the last corner and Leo said, "We're here."

The blue light entered the cavern before them. There was no chill air to greet them like when Marco and Sarah had first found the entrance. Marco figured it was because Leo was with him. They continued into the vast room with all the containers.

Marco immediately felt a clench in his gut at the sight of all those trapped creatures. Even though he knew Leo would take good care of them on his planet, if they made it there, the sight still freaked him out. Especially since he personally knew one of the frozen. His chest tightened as he saw the module that held Sarah's dad. He needed to get John out of there, not only for Sarah, but also his mom. For what he hoped was the last time, Marco set the chest down. He wiped his sweaty hands on his shirt, walked up to the frosty glass, and blew on it. Slowly, a patch cleared and he set his eye to it. John was there, same as before. "Can we let my stepdad out now?"

Leo stepped over to the module and reached for the keypad.

Near the bottom of the module, Marco noticed a steady green light he hadn't seen before. "What's that?"

Leo sucked in a breath and quickly stepped back. "We need to wait until morning."

Marco shook his head. "We need to do this *now* so we can get back to my mom and the others. They need us."

Leo looked nervous. "I agree. But . . . but we need the night to rest." Leo headed toward the end of the cavern.

"Wait!" Marco followed. "You said the freezing process would be complete in less than a day. Don't we need to let him out now?"

Leo didn't answer and kept walking.

Marco grabbed the boy's shoulder. "What's that green light? Why are you acting so weird?"

Leo said, "It's nothing."

But Marco could tell by the sound of his voice that it was anything but. He turned to look at John's module again, and noticed similar lights on the bottom of all the modules. But the others were a steady red. The ones on the modules that had housed Nacho and Ahab were blinking green.

"What do the lights mean, Leo?" Marco had to get

John out and would do whatever it took. "Let him out or I'll drag the chest out of here, right now! You can't back out of our deal."

Leo frowned. "I'm not backing out. But when I said it was about timing, it was more than just getting back to your camp to help your mom."

Marco went and picked up one end of the chest.

"Please!" Leo walked briskly over to Marco, stopping a few feet away. "Listen. The lights . . ." He set a hand on his forehead. "I'm so stupid. I didn't notice them. I forgot."

"Forgot what?" Marco dropped the chest.

Leo lowered his hand. "The containers have to be refilled."

"What do you mean 'refilled'?" Marco did not like the way things were sounding. "Like they have to *go back in*?"

"*Something* has to go back in," said Leo.

"Or what happens?" asked Marco.

"It's over. The automatic shutdown happens and the ship will never leave." Leo sighed.

Marco frowned. "You said the extra containers don't count toward the final tally."

Leo waved his hand toward a bank of empty modules. "Those don't." He pointed at Ahab's, Nacho's, and John's. "But the ones I filled do."

"Once you let them out, how long do you have?"

"About twenty Earth hours."

Nacho and Ahab had already been out for a few hours. Marco asked, "Do you trust me?"

Leo met his stare. "Do you trust *me*?"

Neither said anything for a moment.

Marco swallowed. Did he trust Leo? He wasn't sure. "I think we have to trust each other. I swear to you, I will get those containers refilled. I'm not sure how or with what, but I swear I will. And then we'll help you fill the others that you need and get you home." He held out his hand.

Leo shook it. "I trust you." A corner of his mouth curved up. "But we need to rest, at least a little. I will trust you if you trust me."

Marco didn't like leaving John frozen any longer than he had to. But he nodded, took a last look at both the chest and the module holding John, and followed Leo out of the cave.

IN THE GALLEY OF THE SPACESHIP, Marco sat down. His arms and legs were heavy, exhausted from hauling the chest. He yawned as his stomach growled. He realized he wouldn't do anyone any good in his condition; he needed to eat and get some sleep because there was no telling what lay ahead of them when they got back to the others. He crossed his arms on the table and set his head on them, for just a moment.

He woke to a hand on his shoulder. "Marco. It will be dawn soon."

Marco jumped up. "We need to go!"

"Eat first." Leo pointed at the plate on the table that held scrambled eggs, toast, hash browns, and sliced strawberries. A large glass of milk sat next to it.

Marco grabbed the milk first and took a long drink. Then he grabbed a fork and dug into the breakfast. With his mouth full, he asked Leo, "Can we make food to bring along for the others?"

"I've taken care of that already." He pointed to a silver container. "I feel much better after sleeping."

Although he was mad at himself for nodding off for so long, Marco realized he did too. As he kept eating, he felt even stronger, ready to face whatever lay ahead of them.

Leo set a small white case down on the table. "I think this will help your mother."

"Thank you." Marco pushed the plate away and

slipped the small case into his pocket. "Can we unfreeze John now?"

Leo nodded, grabbed the silver container of food, and hurried with Marco to the cavern.

As they reached the module holding John, Marco said, "Don't take this the wrong way, but you might want to go back to your Earth-boy face? Just for the, um, introductions?"

Immediately, Leo's face morphed into that of the boy Marco had first met. One hand stayed webbed, and he set it on the keypad.

Hssssssssssss.

Mist blew out, sending goose bumps up Marco's arms.

Marco waved both hands about to disperse the cloud.

Seconds later, John stepped out, a bewildered expression on his face. He stumbled and braced himself against the side of the module. Then he took off his glasses and wiped them on his shirt. He replaced them, blinking several times as if to clear his vision. "Marco? Where's Sarah?"

"She's fine," Marco blurted. "She's back at the camp with Mom."

His stepfather relaxed, until he took in his surroundings. "Where am I?" He noticed Leo and pointed at him. "Who are you?"

Marco stepped between Leo and John. "There's a lot we have to tell you. Basically, everything Cash told us was true. But right now we have to go back to camp. Fast. I'll explain on the way."

John frowned at the boys. "Okay. Let's go. But you'd better tell me everything. Now which way is out?"

Leo pointed and John headed that way. Marco noticed that John was limping slightly, like he had some kinks to work out.

Leo touched Marco's arm. "Everything depends on this. My planet. My entire people's existence."

Marco gulped. He had to wait a moment before he had enough breath to say, "I'll figure it out. I promise. We'll be back as soon as we can."

Leo gave him a curt nod and handed him the silver container.

Marco wanted so badly to come through for the stranded alien boy and his people. But he had no idea how he was going to do that. His family was top priority. He would make sure his mom was safe. And the others. Then, and only then, would he try to help Leo out. Because he did mean to try or he wouldn't have promised. But he didn't want to think about what might happen if—when—he failed to live up to that promise.

17

Sarah opened her eyes to a faint pink line across the sky and Ahab's cold nose in her face. She pushed him away gently, then yawned and sat up, stretching her arms above her head. Her body was stiff from sleeping on the sand, and she wondered when she would ever get to sleep in a real bed again. She checked on Yvonna. Her forehead was hot, but she seemed to be resting peacefully. Cash was still asleep too. Nacho's towel was empty.

Sarah jumped to her feet. Should she go look for him? But what happened if Cash or Yvonna needed her while she was gone? So she stayed there, petting Ahab, waiting for Nacho to come back or one of the others to wake up. She finally heard the other girl yawn. "It's almost sunup. We made it."

"Don't speak so soon."

Cash shot straight up as Sarah whirled around at the strange male voice.

The man who stood over them had a yellow-toothed grin that was seedy and vile. As he chewed on a twig stuck in the corner of his mouth, Sarah immediately guessed who he was. A glance at Cash's stricken face confirmed it. The man there in dirty navy-blue shorts, mirrored aviator glasses, and a stupid-looking white safari hat was the one who had taken Sarge's boat. He was Fox, the man who had stranded Cash, all alone, on the island. What kind of a person would do that?

Ahab barked.

Sarah's heart pounded. She suddenly realized— convinced without a doubt—that she and the rest were in deep, deep trouble.

Cash's eyes met Sarah's.

Sarah swallowed her gasp. Cash had her sight back!

Cash asked, "Where's my grandpa?"

The man pointed to the water. "On his boat. Tied up at the moment. I don't trust him *that* much."

Sarah sat there, unsure what to do. She looked down

at the beach, where the bend went out of sight. Could she count on Marco and Leo to be back with her dad soon? They said they'd hurry and try to be back early in the morning.

Maybe she and Cash just needed to talk to this guy for a little while.

Maybe her dad was almost there.

Maybe he was down there, just around the corner, waiting.

"So, who do we have here?" The man was standing over Yvonna, looking down at her in a way that made Sarah very uncomfortable.

"That's my mom," said Sarah.

The man raised his eyebrows. Before he could say anything about them not looking a thing alike, Sarah added, "I'm adopted."

"So how did you end up here?" The man plucked the twig out of his mouth and ran one end along his gruesome teeth.

Sarah faked a cough, giving herself a moment to think. She didn't dare mention the rest of them. She hoped that Nacho knew enough to stay away. She said, "My mom and I were on a sailing trip." She pointed to the wreck of the *Moonflight*, still sitting in the lagoon.

The man nodded as he gazed that way. "You expect

me to believe just the two of you sailed that all the way here?"

"No," said Sarah. "We had a skipper. We hit a really bad storm and he—" Unbidden, the tears welled up in her eyes as she let the memory of that night wash over her. From then on, it was simple to sound believable. "He got washed overboard. And we couldn't do anything but ride it out." She pointed to the lagoon. "We ended up here, the boat stuck on that rock."

The man kicked at the dwindling fire, sending sparks into the air. "You made a fire?"

Sarah glanced at Cash. "She already had it going." Before he could ask more, she offered, "And she helped us haul stuff from the boat. Set up camp."

The man stared down at Cash with heavy lids. "Yeah, she's resourceful, that one."

Cash said, "And they shared their food with me. Since I didn't *have any*."

"Now, now. It's only been a few days." The man tapped on the brim of his hat with a dirty knuckle, tipping it up slightly.

"Did you find your treasure?" asked Cash.

Sarah shot her a look. Why would she bring that up?

The man shook his head. "We're gonna head farther out. But, your grandfather refused to go any farther until we checked on you." He shrugged. "Believe me, if I could handle that boat by myself, he'd be fish food."

Cash's eyes narrowed and her hands turned into fists.

Sarah said, "Could you please call for help for us? My mom is sick and we need to get home."

The man made a clicking sound with his tongue. "Yeah, now . . . that is not gonna happen. See, I'm trying to keep a low profile. And the last thing I need is more people who can identify me. You understand?"

Sarah didn't want to be around this man anymore, but if they left, there was no telling when someone else might come along. "I promise, I won't say anything."

"And I *promise* to give you a ride home." The man laughed. "Sorry, sweetheart. You and your mom will just have to stay here. Maybe when we get back to Fiji I'll put in a call." He glanced at Cash. "Let's go."

Cash crossed her arms and widened her stance. "No. I'm not leaving."

Suddenly, the man's demeanor became tense. He grabbed Cash's arm.

"Ow!"

Ahab barked.

"I said we're going and we're going." He began to drag her across the sand.

"Leave her alone!" Sarah ran after him and grabbed his arm, trying to get him to let go of Cash. He shoved her away, and she landed on her butt in the sand.

Ahab barked again and moved between Fox and Sarah.

The man whirled and kicked at the dog.

"No!" Sarah crawled in front of Ahab and threw her hands up. "Don't hurt him."

Fox shook his head and continued to drag a struggling Cash. "Please! My mom is sick and needs help," gasped Sarah. As he kept walking, she couldn't help herself. "What kind of person are you?"

The man stopped and faced her. "You're right. What kind of person would I be . . ." He set his free hand on his chest, most presumably over his heart, if he even had one, thought Sarah. ". . . if I left an ill woman and her daughter here on a deserted island."

Sarah held her breath. Was he going to take them? What if he did? They couldn't leave without her dad and Marco and Nacho! Then what would she do?

Still gripping Cash's arm, the man bent over Yvonna and picked up a corner of the blanket. He began to drag her.

Sarah froze. Not only was he taking Cash, he was

also taking Yvonna. "No!" She raced after him and grabbed the other end of the blanket and yanked. "We're not going with you!"

The man's hands were full, so he kicked out with his foot, landing a blow straight in Sarah's stomach.

She doubled over and dropped to her knees, the wind knocked out of her.

Fox growled, "Sorry, sweetheart. But you're not invited."

She gasped, trying to get a breath as Ahab licked her face. Tears filled her eyes, and when she could finally squeak in some air, she watched as the man hauled Yvonna and Cash toward the water. Cash looked backward at Sarah, fear in her eyes.

Then her eyes shifted high and to the right.

Sarah turned around.

Nacho's head peeked over the edge of the platform in the trees, his mouth gaping, eyes wide. Sarah gave him a swift shake of her head. He could do nothing to help them. Better that he remained safe to tell her dad and Marco what happened.

Sarah sucked in another breath as she held her stomach. She had to do something to keep that sailboat from leaving with Yvonna and Cash. She had to stall the man long enough for Marco and Leo to get back with her dad.

And then she knew. There was only one thing that would keep that man from leaving.

She waited another moment until she had her breath back, then called out, "You really should stay! This island is cool!"

The man ignored her as he dragged the blanket with Yvonna in one hand and yanked Cash with the other.

Cash stared back at her.

Louder, Sarah yelled, "There's even a rock that LOOKS LIKE A FACE!"

The man froze. He dropped his hold on the blanket and let go of Cash. She fell to the sand and then scrambled away from him.

Fox turned back toward Sarah.

"What did you say?"

Sarah was still shaky, but got to her feet. Holding Ahab's collar, she bravely took a few steps closer to Fox so she wouldn't have to yell to be heard. "This island. It's pretty cool."

The man looked annoyed. "After that."

Sarah swallowed. "There's a rock that looks like a face. We call it the *face rock.*"

His mouth dropped open for a moment, then closed, the corners turning up into a not-very-nice smile. "Yeah, sweetheart. I'm gonna need you to show that to me."

Sarah shrugged. "I don't know. It depends on whether you are going to help me or not."

The man strode toward her.

She cringed, but stood her ground.

He got so close she could smell his cheap cologne. He reached out and snatched one of her braids. He wrapped it around his hand and pulled, not quite hard enough that it hurt, but definitely hard enough so that she couldn't move away from him.

"Where's that rock? I need you to take me there, *now*."

Even though she wasn't sure she could find it, she nodded.

He let go of her braid. "Well, okay then." He spun around on one heel and walked briskly toward Cash. "Change in plans, doll. We're staying."

Sarah's knees almost gave out. She set a shaking hand on her pounding heart. She'd done it. She'd kept him from leaving with Yvonna. But she also realized that now this horrible stranger was staying.

And until Marco and Leo showed up with her dad, she would be under the control of the man who abandoned Cash on the island.

If he'd leave a defenseless girl alone on a remote island, there's no telling what else he would do.

Sarah went over to check on Yvonna, who was still asleep or maybe even unconscious. What if she was even worse? She had to keep that man away from her stepmother, and stall until the others got there.

She needed a plan, and there was only one that made any sense.

Sarah would have to show him the way to the face rock.

But what if that's where he had left his treasure? What would happen to her when he realized it was gone?

She could only hope that her dad found her before then. Because if he didn't . . .

A warm breeze blew her way. And despite its promise of a sweltering day, Sarah shivered.